You're Not Supposed to Cry

Gary Duncan

Vagabond Voices
Glasgow

First published on 26 May 2017 by
Vagabond Voices Publishing Ltd.,
Glasgow,
Scotland.
ISBN 978-1-908251-80-0

Printed and bound in Poland

Cover design by Mark Mechan

Typeset by Park Productions

The publisher acknowledges subsidy towards
this publication from Creative Scotland

ALBA | CHRUTHACHAIL

For further information on Vagabond Voices, see the website,
www.vagabondvoices.co.uk

For Claudia, Livia and Max

Contents

You're Not
Supposed to Cry

Snap

He was James when they met, before he became Jim and then Big Jim. Stick-insect James, too tall and too thin, always ducking through doorways, always minding his head.

Melissa told him he looked like an exclamation mark. A good thing, too, because she'd always seen herself as a full stop, short and squat. A match made in heaven, she'd said, or if not heaven then somewhere else.

Their first night, helping him out of his trousers, Melissa whispered she'd be gentle, that she wouldn't hurt him, this being his first time and this not being anywhere near her first time. She didn't see the point in lying to him about that. Us full stops, she'd said, shrugging her round shoulders, we don't pick and choose.

Horizontal, with his underpants bunched around his spindly ankles, she thought he was more like an elongated dash than an exclamation mark: brittle, vulnerable, something she could snap in two with her bare hands.

Now, curled up like a comma, the bruises still fresh, she thinks back to that night all those years ago, before James became Jim and Jim became Big Jim, before he stopped pretending to be someone he wasn't.

She closes her eyes and tries to remember what it used to be like. She hears him banging doors downstairs, the TV blaring, and wishes she'd snapped him in two when she'd had the chance.

A Fairly Decent Proposal

Ellen said a guy at work had offered her four hundred quid to sleep with her.

"A bit like that film," she said, "you know, the one with Robert Redford and Demi Moore."

They'd come to the end of the track and looked left and right, rolling fields in every direction.

"I think we're lost," Tony said.

Ellen took out her map. She'd left her glasses in the car and had to squint at it.

"Left," she said.

"Are you sure?"

They walked a mile or so and Tony said, "Who is it? This guy."

"John."

"John in IT?"

Ellen nodded.

Tony nodded.

He'd met John a couple of times. Nice guy. Late twenties, he guessed. Goatee. A good-looking guy.

"He's a good-looking guy," Tony said.

"He is. He's sweet. He does triathlons. Runs to work every day, swims and rides his bike at lunchtime."

"So what did he say? He just comes right out and says it? That he'd like to sleep with you?"

"More or less. He popped round to look at my

printer and we got talking, about work and things, you know, and he just comes right out and says it. Says I hope you don't mind."

Ellen stopped and took out her water bottle. She took a sip, then another, then offered it to Tony.

"We can stop here and have some coffee," Tony said, looking around. The wind had died down and the grass was long and soft, but still wet underfoot. "Nice spot."

"I said I'd think about it," Ellen said. "Said I'd sleep on it, if you pardon the pun. And run it by you."

Tony said, "Four hundred quid?"

Ellen nodded.

"Four hundred quid," Tony repeated. "That's not to be sniffed at."

"That's what I thought."

"Quite generous really, when you think about it."

"We could put it towards the holiday fund."

"Or get the boiler sorted out."

Ellen took off her rucksack and rolled her shoulders. She unclipped the pedometer from the waistband of her waterproof trousers. They'd walked about four miles and still had another four or five to go. More if they were lost.

"I was thinking," she said. "About it. John's a nice guy, and reasonable. How about we suggest five hundred?"

"*Five* hundred?"

"Or maybe six."

"That's quite a lot of money."

"I know."

"I don't think we should be too ... you know, pushy."

Ellen reached into her rucksack for the flask. "Maybe you're right," she said.

"Or disrespectful. To John."

"Tell you what," Ellen said, unscrewing the lid, "why don't I have a word with him tomorrow."

"I think that would make sense."

"Just have a quick word with him. See if there's any wiggle room."

A Good Listener

He heated some tinned soup and buttered three slices of bread, the cheap stuff Pam had refused to buy because it used to get stuck to the roof of her mouth.

He washed up — bowl, pan, knife and spoon — and got the tape ready, propping it up against a cushion on the sofa, on Pam's side. He sat down next to it and pressed play.

He used to take a notepad and pen with him, on buses and trains, in the café, in the park. He'd get as close as he could, close enough to listen without raising suspicion. He was a lonely old man, and people weren't too suspicious of lonely old men, but he was careful nonetheless. You had to be, these days.

Sometimes he'd fill five, ten pages, scribbling till his arthritic old hands ached: snatches of other people's conversations, family problems, work gossip, dinner plans, doctor's appointments.

It was much easier now, with the tape recorder: all he had to do was press the record button and sit back. No frantic scribbling, no clumsy turning of pages. Later, at home, no straining his eyes as he tried to decipher his messy notes.

*

The tape crackled and he waited anxiously. Things often went wrong. He'd forget to press record, the ribbon would unspool and he'd have to unpick it with a pencil. Sometimes he'd end up chucking it into the bin — an afternoon wasted.

This time, it worked. He listened, nodded, interjected, but mostly just listened. Once or twice he paused the tape and tried to pick up the conversation: tried to chip in with a humorous anecdote or a pithy put-down, or ramble on like Pam used to do. But the words never came out right. He was a listener, not a talker. It wasn't the same now, without her, but it was something.

Better than This

Rita left me with the baby. There was a baby. She'd never mentioned anything about a baby.

*

She was on her way out. Standing in front of the broken gas fire, looking down at me. I was on the sofa, settled down for what I thought was going to be a night in. Just the two of us.

"What would you give me?" she asks, pursing her lips.

"Give you?"

"Out of ten. Marks out of ten."

She strikes a pose, hands on hips.

"What?" I say. "I don't know. Nine maybe."

She looks down at herself, at the acres of cleavage.

"Not a ten?"

"Maybe a ten, I don't know, I—"

She turns back to the mirror and applies more cherry-red lipstick.

"Would you fuck me?" she says. "Imagine you've just met me and you see me, like this. Would you fuck me?"

"I *have* just met you."

"You know what I mean."

"Yes," I say, "I *would* fuck you."

She seems happy with that, and blows me a kiss in the mirror.

She steps back and gives herself a final once-over before making for the door.

"He should sleep for a couple of hours, the baby, but you might have to feed him later," she says.

*

I met her earlier that day, at the greasy spoon. She was wearing a dirty-grey uniform with egg stains down the front.

She gave me an extra sausage and sat down opposite me, even though there were customers waiting and her boss kept giving her sideways looks, muttering under his breath.

"Do you want to come round sometime?" she asked. "My place." She reached for my coffee and took a tiny sip.

"Okay," I said. "I'd like that."

"How about tonight? You're not doing anything tonight, are you?" She didn't wait, and scribbled her address down on the little notepad she used to take the orders. "Seven o'clock," she said.

*

"You could have mentioned the baby," I say when she wakes me up. I'm back on the sofa, rubbing the gunk from my eyes.

She's at the mirror again, only now she's in her dressing gown and her make-up's smudged, her hair tatty and greasy.

"I thought you knew," she says, giggling.

"Knew what? I only just met you and you forgot to mention the fact that you have a baby. You think you might have said something about that? That you wanted me to *babysit?*"

I get up, a little unsteady on my feet. "What time is it?"

She says, "Eight, I think, or maybe nine, I don't know," and turns and disappears into the bedroom, a sweet, stale trail of perfume and beer and cigarettes behind her.

*

She makes me a coffee and we sit in the cramped kitchenette. It's the same cheap coffee from the greasy spoon, and when she sees the look on my face she shrugs and says, "Perks of the job." She reaches over and opens a cupboard to reveal three industrial-size tins of the stuff and five or six bottles of cheap ketchup.

"They pay me shit," she says, "so I take what I can." She grins. "Just enough to get by, you know."

After our second cup, she says, "So how was he? Did he sleep right through?"

"He was crying."

"Babies do that."

"He was crying a lot."

"Ah, poor little thing, he was probably hungry."

"I couldn't find anything. Baby food, baby stuff. Just some spaghetti hoops."

She's smiling.

"What?"

"Spaghetti hoops?"

"And some toast. I mashed it all up with a fork. He seemed to like it."

*

The kid had sat in my arms, glassy-eyed and docile, dribbling from the corner of his mouth. When I tried to take him back into the bedroom, he cried again and grabbed my finger.

I nodded off at one point. When I woke up, he was still watching me, still holding my finger.

When he finally closed his eyes, I whispered, "Sleep tight, little man. You deserve better than this."

*

Halfway through the third cup of coffee, a guy appears in the doorway. Yawning. Naked.

"All right," he says to me, scratching himself.

I nod, and watch as he walks over to the sink and pours himself a glass of water.

He knocks it back in one, and turns and leans against the sink.

"You live here?" he says to me.

I look away. "No."

Rita places her cold hand on mine and says, "Freddy, meet Sam. Sam, meet Freddy."

Freddy offers his hand, the same hand he was scratching himself with.

We shake. His hand's warmer than Rita's, and clammier.

"I'm going back to bed," Freddy says, yawning again.

Rita gets up.

"Good idea," she says and ruffles my hair on the way out.

Black and Blue

He forgets things now: where he parked the car, where he left his keys, his glasses, his phone. Birthdays, names, faces.

Sometimes, lying in bed and staring up at the cob-webbed ceiling, he doesn't even know what day it is. He thinks it might be Tuesday today. It feels like Tuesday. Or maybe Wednesday. He rolls over on to his side and tries to figure it out, working backwards. But he only confuses himself further, the days blurring into one.

He gets up, slowly. His head's not quite right, all light and fuzzy, like it belongs to someone else. He's not old — he's not old or young, he's somewhere in the middle — but he's started to shuffle, to drag his feet over the threadbare carpet. He thinks this is what it's going to be like when he is old, only worse.

In the bathroom he runs the cold tap, cupping his hands, splashing the water against his face. It's cold enough to take his breath away, and sometimes that helps when he can't remember: a short, sharp shock.

Something clicks in his head. A moment of clarity, fleeting but real. It's Tuesday, it's *definitely* Tuesday. He splashes more water in his face, spilling it over the side of the basin, on to the floor.

He likes Tuesdays. On Tuesdays he tidies the house,

does some washing, some gardening, some pottering. Tuesdays, he remembers, are bin days, the chance to clear everything out, unburden himself and start again. This is a good thing, he thinks, but he can't remember if it's black or blue bin day today. He has a feeling it's black, but then he thinks it might be blue. Black or blue: the only thing he knows for certain is that it's one or the other.

He dries his face with a cloth and looks out of the window. He sees the bins at the bottom of the garden, black and blue, side by side next to the fence. One for general waste, one for recycling. He used to have a brown one, too, but he can't remember what that was for, or what happened to it.

He stands on his tiptoes and cranes his neck to look down the road. It's still early and the road is binless. Not a bin in sight. This confuses him because the old woman across the road (she's a friend, he thinks, but he can't for the life of him remember her name) likes to get her bin out early, usually the night before. Sometimes he can hear her, dragging the bin down the path, the wheels squeaking, but he can't remember hearing anything last night or this morning. She's old, much older than he is, and she hasn't been well. He wonders if she's all right, wonders if she might have slipped quietly away through the night. He hopes not because he likes her, even though he still can't remember her name.

He ponders this as he shuffles back to the bedroom. His head is spinning, a prickly heat washing over him. He has another moment of clarity: sometime in the not too distant past, hunched over his desk, he'd made a list, a list of bin days. He'd circled the days, the alternate Tuesdays, in black and blue, so he wouldn't forget. He'd smiled: a little victory.

He lies down now and squints up at the ceiling and tries to remember what he did with the list.

It Waits

It sits, and waits for her. Quiet except for the odd gurgle and creak and rumble as it settles down for the day.

She just left, and won't be back for hours. It can still hear her footsteps on the garden path, the clank of the rusty metal gate.

She's new, this one. They haven't got to know each other yet, not properly, but it likes her.

Not like the last lot. The noise they made, the mess. All that banging and hammering and shouting. Then nothing, after they moved out, and that was almost as bad as having them around. Those long, interminable days of nothing.

It likes to watch her. It watches her all the time, when she's sleeping, when she's in the shower, when she's sitting in the armchair by the window, thinking, looking out.

It thinks she might be lonely. She doesn't seem to have many friends. An older woman came round when she first moved in, but just the once. It thinks the older woman might have been her mother, but it's not sure. And there was that man, the man with the overnight bag. Came prepared, but didn't stay long. They'd argued and he left, just like that, half-way through the pizza they'd ordered. Took his bag with him and almost kicked a hole in the door on his way out.

She didn't cry, not till he was gone, and then it watched her sob and heave and later, much later, fall asleep on the sofa.

But it knows she's going to be okay. Next morning it watched her shower and make breakfast, humming a happy song to herself as she got ready for work.

Yes, it thinks, she's going to be okay. We're both going to be okay.

It settles down and listens to its own familiar rhythms, its gurgling pipes and creaking joists. It waits, and knows it's nothing without her, nothing but bricks and mortar.

Floral Notes

She makes a pot of coffee, that Ethiopian muck she likes, the one with the "floral notes" and "refreshing citrusy zing". He's told her before about that, that he doesn't like that shit at all, not one little bit. That it tastes like topsoil. She apologises and says she'll try to get some of the Brazilian blend he likes for next time, the nutty one with the caramel overtones, but he thinks the damage might already have been done. That there's only so much he can take and that all things considered she's being a little bit fucking presumptuous if she thinks there's even going to *be* a next time.

Crepuscular

She'd been standing there the night before, at the window.

"I love this time of night," she'd said. "All ... *crepuscular*."

He didn't reply, so she said, "Twilight. Early evening. It's one of my favourite words." Then, looking straight at him, "It means *dim*."

Now he was looking out of the window.

"It's getting dark," he said.

He was dressed and shaved and wearing the new shoes she'd bought him, but he didn't want to go out. He didn't do dinner parties.

She'd insisted on them, the shoes. Black, Italian, expensive.

Nice enough shoes, he thought, but not him.

"Too tight," he'd said to the bloke in the shop. He took a ten, wide. He had his dad's feet, big and flat, like paddles.

But she'd waved him away, said they were meant to be like that. Snug. The bloke in the shop didn't seem so sure, but shrugged and said, "Don't worry, they'll be fine once you've worn them in."

He'd put his foot down with the tie, though. He didn't do ties either.

They'd talked about it earlier and she'd said, "You

wear the tie, or we're done." He thought she was joking, but there she was, ready to go, the tie in her hand.

"You said you would," she said.

"I didn't."

Maybe he did. She'd said she'd do that thing to him in the shower if he wore the tie.

"You'll be the odd one out," she said, throwing the tie at him. "Hurry fucking up."

He'd told his friends about her. Way, way out of my league, he'd said. And loaded. But cold, cold as fuck. He'd liked that at first, the way she treated him, that air she had about her. The way she talked to him, the big words.

"Who wears a fucking tie for dinner?" he said and turned back towards the window.

His feet ached.

"Come on," she said, softer, "let's go."

He looked out, watched as grey turned to black. He didn't know how long he stood there, but when he turned back she was gone, the tie still on the floor.

Peachy

Ian mulls it over on the way back home, how the word had just popped right out like that, ambushing him. He doesn't know what to make of it, and he's more than a little confused. He takes the long way back, through the park, across the football field, hoping the cold wind and the extra mile and a half will help settle him, help clear his befuddled head.

"Hello," she'd said, scanning the tin of peas he'd picked up from the reduced aisle. He'd said hello back to her, as you do, and hoped that would be the end of it. Or maybe that's what had thrown him: the hope that that wouldn't be the end of it. She's new. New and young and alive and not like the other ones who usually serve him: the large Asian lady, the scowling assistant manager, the old guy with the sweaty armpits. Maybe that was it, because she's new. Or maybe it's her cheekbones, or the snug uniform.

"How's your day so far?" she'd said, looking up at him, bright-eyed and full of everything that was good and young and beautiful and, for him, unattainable.

"Peachy," he'd said. There it was. Out there, before he could do anything about it. He knew he'd have to apologise, immediately and profusely: that he'd have to tell the cashier with the cheekbones and the snug uniform that he didn't know what had come over him, that he's not the kind of person who goes around using words like "peachy".

But she'd nodded and said, "That's great. In fact I'm feeling pretty peachy myself too."

He thinks of all the other things he could have said, or should have said, as she scanned the rest of his items: the microwave shepherd's pie, the tin of tomato soup, the small white loaf.

"Thank you," he said, because there was nothing else to say. He took his change and left, and didn't look back.

Body Parts

Jan emptied her bag on to the sand.

It was a decent haul — a rubber glove, a half-eaten apple, a plastic lighter — but Michael was more interested in the discarded pasty he'd spotted near the dunes. He'd found a prosthetic leg last week (with sock still attached) and hadn't stopped talking about it since. How he'd taken it into Seahouses, to the police station, and the sergeant behind the desk had said, "What's that then?" and Michael had said, "It's a leg," and the desk sergeant had said, "Oh all right, you'd better hand it over then."

Michael got his photo in the paper the next week and was told he could keep the leg (and sock) if no one claimed it within six months.

Jan looked down at her haul and stormed off, in search of her own body parts.

Diversionary Purchases

The security guard smiles at her on her way in. She imagines him spread-eagled on her bed, whimpering, but he's big, probably too big for her, so she keeps her head down and moves on.

There's a CCTV camera on her right, in Paints. There's another one in the next aisle and another in the garden tool section at the far end of the store. Probably lots more she isn't even aware of. She tries to ignore them, to go about her business like a normal person.

She picks up a few things she doesn't need, what she likes to call diversionary purchases — a light bulb, a new brush head — and makes her way to Tapes and Packaging. She feels that little flutter in her chest when she gets to Tiles and Flooring: almost there. And then she sees it, all that tape laid out in front of her. A whole shelf, newly stocked, like they'd been expecting her.

She reaches for a roll of heavy-duty, low-noise PVC. The good stuff: 50 microns, 50 mils. She resists the temptation to sniff it. She takes another roll, and a roll of Economy Brown. She's not sure about the Economy: it may very well be versatile and cost-effective, as it says on the poorly printed label, but it's only 40 microns and she thinks tear resistance might be an issue, not to mention tangle-free unwinding. She turns it over in her hand and gives it a gentle squeeze. It's a little on the squishy side, so she puts it back on the shelf. Versatile and cost-effective are all fine and well, but the last thing she needs are untangling issues when she's got some angry fucking brute thrashing around underneath her.

The Woods

Frank stopped where the bridge used to be, and looked around.

"It's all gone," he said. "The bridge, the stream."

Mike looked back the way they'd come: row after row of red-brick houses with red-tiled roofs and red-paint doors. They'd parked the van on the edge of the estate and walked through another development: more red-brick houses with red-tiled roofs and red-paint doors.

"It must have been something," Mike said. "Before all this."

He took a bottle of water from his rucksack and offered it to Frank. Frank needed something stronger, but he took it, clumsily, and spilled most of it down his chin. The others had stayed back a little, but they were watching him: eight pairs of eyes boring into him.

"We can wait here a bit," Mike said. "Till you catch your breath."

"I'm fine," Frank said.

They set off into the woods, the path forking left and right and then petering out. Frank took his time, breathing in the cool, damp air: the sweet smell of wet soil and fallen leaves that took him back to another time.

He stopped when they reached the clearing and looked up at the light filtering in through the tops of the trees.

"Here?" Mike asked.

Frank shook his head. He inhaled, held it and let it out slowly. "I'd almost forgotten that smell."

Mike looked back towards the path.

"Jesus Christ," he said, grinding his boot into a pile of dead leaves.

One of the guards had lost a shoe in the mud and was trying to retrieve it with a moss-covered branch. He was young, about the same age as Frank last time he'd been in the woods, all those years ago.

"Maybe you should help," Frank said.

"Maybe he should watch where he's fucking walking."

Mike bent down and grabbed some leaves.

"Why now, Frank? Why wait all this time?"

Frank shrugged. "I don't know. Maybe it's just the right time. The right thing to do."

Mike threw the leaves up in the air and watched them fall slowly back to the ground, turning, caught in the breeze.

Frank looked down at his hands.

"How about taking these things off, Mike?"

"You know I can't do that."

Frank nodded. Mike was one of the good ones. He understood.

They set off again when the others reached the clearing: Frank out front, Mike one step behind, the others following.

Frank could have cut through the bramble bushes,

28

like he'd done the last time, but he didn't want to make it too easy for them. Let them sweat a bit first. They'd waited long enough: another hour wouldn't make much difference.

He took them away from the clearing, farther into the woods, down to where the stream used to run deep and wide. Every now and then he slowed down and looked back and saw them all lined up behind him, single file on the narrow path.

When they'd almost gone full circle, Mike came up beside him and said, "I know what you're doing, Frank."

Frank ignored him.

"Frank, you—"

"They're over there," Frank said. "Other side of the bramble bushes. I killed them both, just like they said, and buried them in the ground, deep in the ground."

Frank looked around one last time. "I'm sorry, Mike. You can take me back now."

Incomparable

"There's probably a big fancy word for it," he says, caressing her ankle.

"For what?" she says.

"For this."

Shelley looks down, her feet on his lap, her shoes and socks on the floor next to the sofa.

He started on her left ankle, the tips of his fingers barely touching: up and down, round and round, figure of eight. He squeezed it once, but apologised, said he didn't mean to hurt her. She said it was fine, in fact it felt quite nice, so he could do it again if he wanted to.

She'd propped herself up on the sofa with a couple of cushions. She reaches back and removes one now, and reclines a little.

He didn't think anyone would reply to the ad. Five months and nothing. Then Shelley contacted him.

"Would you mind if I did the other one?" he asks.

He waits, his hand hovering.

"Please," she says. She's blushing.

She'd sent him a photo, as he'd requested in the ad. He'd left an email address, his preferred method of communication, but the photo arrived in the post. First class, in a hard-backed envelope. A slightly fuzzy close-up of her ankles.

*

His second wife, Patricia, had lovely ankles: so small, so delicate, so out of kilter with the rest of her, with her meaty calves and lumpy thighs. But he knew, as soon as he saw that photo, that Shelley was the one, the one he'd been waiting for.

He starts on the other ankle. Same as before, with the tips of his fingers, up and down, round and round, figure of eight. A gentle squeeze.

Shelley had offered to take her trousers off: said she didn't mind, if it made it easier for him. But he'd said no, the trousers should stay on, the trousers should definitely stay on, so she'd turned the bottoms up, three or four times till they were just above the knee.

He'd called her after seeing the photo. Said they should meet in the park, somewhere out in the open, because there were some very odd people about these days and you couldn't be too careful. There were picnic tables, he said, near the duck pond. They could sit there, pretend they were just like a normal couple.

She said she'd rather meet at his place: she didn't like parks, or duck ponds, or big open spaces. Lots of other things, she said, her voice cracking, but that was another story.

"What do you think?" she asks.

He pauses and looks up at her.

"Think?"

"My ankles. Only, I've never thought they were anything out of the ordinary. Anything special."

"Shelley," he says, "you have no idea." He looks down again and closes his eyes, and they all come back to him: every ankle he's ever fondled or caressed, every ankle he's ever admired or coveted from afar. And not just the thin ones, the toned ones, the athletic ones, but all of them, the fat ones, the hairy ones, the knobbly ones, the pierced and tattooed ones. Patricia's too: the benchmark, the ankles he kept on loving even after he'd fallen out of love with the rest of her.

He opens his eyes.

"Yours," he says, trying to find the words. "They're incomparable."

Shelley smiles. She wiggles her toes and blushes again. She reaches for the other cushion and lies back, her head on the armrest. "They're all yours," she says.

Mirror Image

The kid's definitely his. The kid's a carbon copy of him, like looking in the mirror: the cockeyes, the sloped forehead, the dimpled chin.

"No getting away from it," Tam says, sliding the photo back over the table. "But he's an ugly little bastard."

Maggie looks at the photo. She smiles to herself and slips the photo back into her pocket.

"How old is he?" Tam asks.

"Nearly three."

Tam thinks back three years, to that one time with Maggie in the storeroom. Her hair's shorter now, shorter and more sensible, but she hasn't changed.

"What's his name?"

"Todd."

"Todd?"

She shrugs.

They never really talked, not after the storeroom. Couple of weeks later, she was gone, quit and moved away.

"So what do you want from me?" he asks.

Another shrug.

"I don't have much," he says.

"Are you still at the warehouse?"

"Eighteen years." He laughs. "If I'd murdered

someone, they'd be letting me out soon." He waits and says, "It's not so bad, you know." He doesn't tell her how much he hates it, how much he's always hated it. He doesn't tell her about his new shift boss, about the early starts and late finishes, about his wife leaving and taking the kids with her.

"I don't want anything off you," she says.

He nods.

"You look like you're doing okay," he says. He'd got there early, took the corner table and watched her pull up in a big black Land Rover. Just her, no kid. He's glad she didn't bring the kid.

"I'm doing okay," she says. He notices the ring, the nice watch.

"Why now?" he says.

"I thought you'd want to know. I thought it was time you knew."

"Let me see the photo again," he says.

She takes it out of her pocket and hands it over to him. He has a closer look. The kid's squinting into the camera, his smile lopsided.

Pity the kid doesn't look more like his mother, he thinks.

"He looks like a nice kid," he says.

Knowing

Sally offered to do it this time, to make them both a nice cup of coffee, but he was already up, shuffling towards the sink, muttering.

"You just sit there and stop fussing," he said, filling the kettle. She watched him, his wiry arms shaking, his gnarled fingers trembling. "You're just like your mother," he said. "She was the same, always fussing, always worrying, even when she was little."

Sally smiled. "She's just looking out for you, Granda. That's all."

Sally leaned forward, her elbows on the table, that big solid lump of a table that he'd fashioned with those arms, those fingers, all those years ago, when he was her age now, when her mother, the worrier, was little.

Looking at him now, framed in the window, hunched over the sink, Sally was struck by how small he'd become, as if he'd been shrinking bit by bit, right before her eyes, and she'd only just noticed: the shirt loose around his neck, the trousers hanging off him, arseless.

He muttered something to himself and turned to plug the kettle in, water spilling out on to the work-top as he fumbled for the switch.

Sally traced a finger over the table, over the

familiar knots and cracks and splits. It was something her mother used to do, something she still did, something passed down.

"I want you to have it," he said. "The table. When I'm gone."

"Granda, you—"

"Bloody thing'll outlive the lot of us," he said, laughing, coughing, turning towards the sink to spit. "Well, me anyway."

Sally didn't like him saying things like that, and he knew it. She usually tried to laugh it off, tell him to hush, stop being a silly old bugger, but he'd give her that look and say, I mean it, Sal, I want you to have it, I want you to know that, and she'd turn away, thinking of all those times they'd gathered round that table, the whole family, the birthdays and Christmases and long Sunday lunches, and she'd nod quietly and whisper back to him, I know you do, her voice breaking.

She watched him spoon the coffee into two chipped mugs, taking his time but spilling some of it anyway, halfway between coffee tin and mug, and not noticing.

She looked away, circling a big black knot in the table with her index finger, trying not to cry. He'd done the same thing last time, had mistaken the gravy granules for the coffee, and she hadn't said anything, couldn't bring herself to say anything, and had forced it down, just a mouthful, lumpy and salty; lukewarm, too, because he'd switched the kettle off before the water had boiled. She'd nursed the mug in her hands, hiding it from him, pretending to sip from it every now and then. Emptied it into the sink later when he wasn't looking.

"Let me help you," she said, getting up. She grabbed the mugs before he could complain, and carried them over to the table.

"I'm thinking of getting back out into the workshop," he said. "Get the old tools out again."

Sally smiled and they talked, and it was almost like old times. Then he asked about Dan, why Dan never came round any more, and she was going to explain to him again, once again, that Dan didn't come around any more because Dan had left her and the boys, their three young boys, but she saw that far-off look in his eyes and knew she'd lost him again, maybe just for a minute, maybe for good, so she'd just shrugged and pretended to take a sip from her mug.

Off-White

She can't see much, not from there. Just the skirting board and the carpet and the patch of wall next to the bedside table. She's close enough to reach out and touch the wall, to see the hairline cracks in the plaster, the smudges and the fingerprints and the thin layer of dust. They haven't decorated for seven or eight years, since Lucy moved out, and it's beginning to show. They talk about it, of doing things, sprucing things up, maybe rearranging the rooms. But that's all it is: talk.

A lick of paint would be a start, Alice thinks. She's never cared much for the off-white, the Evening Barley. That had been Dave's idea. Nice and neutral, he'd said. Nothing too vibrant. And none of that white-white stuff. He'd made a face, just in case she hadn't got the message. So they'd gone for the Evening Barley, the off-white. A hint of yellow. Alice thought it looked dirty, like day-old bathwater.

Raspberry, she thinks, shifting her weight on to one elbow. She shakes her free hand, feels the pins and needles creeping up her forearm. Yes, she thinks: a shock of raspberry, something fiery, in-your-face.

She hears him grunt. She's almost forgotten about him. Another grunt, like he's trying to clear his throat.

"Okay?" she asks, half turning, looking back.

He nods vigorously, eyes tight shut, and digs his fingernails into the huge fleshy expanse of her backside.

"Almost there," he says.

Alice turns back to the wall, to the skirting board and the carpet. Raspberry, she thinks. Definitely raspberry.

On Reflection We've Decided
We're Going to Keep You

Alan sits in the hallway while his parents talk about him in the living room.

Mum said they wouldn't be long, and has given him some magazines to read while he waits. *Woman's Weekly*. *Auto Trader*.

"Look at you!" she'd said before she went in. "Like you're waiting to see the dentist!"

Alan tried to smile, but it didn't come out right.

Mum had called the meeting the previous week. She'd written him a letter and slipped it under his bedroom door. Nothing to be alarmed about, she said, but they needed to have a talk.

He'd asked about it the next morning at breakfast.

"Not really a talk," she'd explained. "More of an … *appraisal*."

*

Alan shifts uncomfortably in his seat. The hallway is cold but he feels clammy, a little breathless.

Mum sticks her head around the door a minute later and smiles.

"You can come in now, darling," she says.

Alan gets up. He straightens his trousers and buttons his jacket. It's his dad's jacket, a couple of sizes too small. Dad suggested he borrow it anyway.

You know what Mum's like, he'd whispered. She'll be pleased you made the effort.

Alan knocks on the door and goes in.

Mum and Dad are sitting on the sofa. Alan's armchair has been pushed into the corner, out of the way, so he sits on the wooden stool they've positioned in the middle of the floor, directly in front of them. One of the legs is shorter than the others, and he rocks back and forwards every time he moves.

"Thanks for coming," Mum says, looking up from her clipboard.

"Sorry for the wait, son," Dad says.

"Alan," Mum says, slowly. "As I explained in my letter, we just wanted to have a little talk, now that you're thirty-seven. Just you and me and Dad."

"A talk?" Alan asks.

Mum nods. "To discuss your ... progress."

"Your progress," Dad repeats.

"But—" Alan starts to say.

Mum gives him that look. She doesn't like being interrupted.

"On the whole, Alan," she says, "we're fairly pleased with you. With the way you've turned out."

Dad nods and clears his throat.

"That's the thing," he says. "With kids. You never quite know what you're going to get."

"Alan," Mum says. "We've given it some thought and we've decided we'd like to keep you."

She gets up and hands the clipboard to Alan.

Alan takes it, not sure exactly what he's supposed to do with it.

"I want you to read through this very carefully," Mum says. "And then sign at the bottom."

Making a Splash

The woman who was supposed to be keeping an eye on him said they were *this* close to calling the police.

"Man of your age," she said, "disappearing like that."

She told him to wait in reception while she let the manager know they'd found him. He looked down at his feet. His slippers were soaked. His socks and trousers too, all the way up to the knee.

When the woman who was supposed to be keeping an eye on him returned and saw the wet patch on the carpet, she muttered to herself and said, "Come on, you old fool, let's get you back to your room before you cause any more trouble."

She offered her arm and he took it, suddenly very tired. When they got back to his room, she put his slippers and socks on the radiator and found a new pair of trousers for him.

"Come on," she said, holding up the trousers, "don't be shy." When she was gone, he shuffled over to the window and looked out across the car park, at all the puddles. He smiled. He'd go round the back next time, down the path, towards the stream. And he'd put his boots on this time.

Safe

Karen rinsed the cups under the cold tap and stared out of the window. It wasn't much of a view, just the overgrown weeds and the broken fence, but it was something, and it could have been worse. She hadn't slept much last night, even with the pills, the wind coming in hard and low over the sea, battering the fence, keeping her awake till the early hours. She'd taken refuge under the blankets, safe in her own little world, and had tried to lull herself back to sleep. This morning she'd stepped outside for a cigarette while she surveyed the damage: another gaping hole in the fence, the contents of the recycling bin — plastic bottles, milk cartons, old newspapers — strewn across the back garden.

"Don't worry about it," Emma said.

They'd sent Emma to look after her, to help her settle in. Karen wasn't sure about her, not yet.

"I'll get someone to look at it," Emma said. "The fence. Should have been fixed anyway, before you moved in." She scribbled something into her notepad, flicked the page over, stared at it for a moment and scribbled something else.

Karen turned back to the window and studied her reflection, the stranger's face looking back at her. They'd done something with her nose, had broken it and rebuilt it. Made it smaller, sharper. She didn't know if she liked it yet, but knew she'd have to live with it. She suddenly thought of her mum and dad, and how much she missed them. Her dad would have made a joke about it, despite everything. About her new nose, her new face. He'd have found the right words, as he always did. Would have taken her by the hand and smiled and said what's done is done, or something like that.

Karen filled the cups. Spilled some of it before she reached the table and stopped and looked down at the mess, not knowing what to do, as Emma jumped up and grabbed an old dishcloth from the sink. Karen watched her mop it up, watched her get down on her hands and knees and give it a good scrub, then inspect the floor, pressing her finger against the ancient, cracked lino, scratching it with a long fingernail.

"We can fix that too," she said, getting to her feet and looking around, at the grimy cupboards and peeling wallpaper. She sat back down at the table and made some more notes. "I'm sorry," she said, shaking her head, "all this should have been done before you moved in."

Karen shrugged. She looked down at the floor, at the damp patch and the ring of dust around it. "You don't have to do this for me," she said. "You know what I've done, you know who I am."

Emma had read the file a dozen times, despite herself. All those files, all those boxes and boxes of files. She'd gone through everything, the court transcripts, the witness statements, the police reports. She'd studied the photos, pored over them, even the ones that had been red-flagged, the ones that were going to stay with her till the day she died.

"I'm here," she said. "I'm here, and that's all that matters for now."

Creatures of Habit

Gordon's at the other end of the patio, peering into the undergrowth, into the tangle of weeds and thistles.

"It's gone," he says, turning and walking back to the table. He's still holding the shovel, just in case.

"I fucking hate frogs," Ruth says, shaking.

"I think it was a toad," Gordon says.

"I don't fucking care what it was."

"Definitely a toad," Gordon says, but he's not sure, not really.

*

He asks Martin about it later. Martin's pretty good with things like that.

"Probably a frog," he says, shrugging.

"Ruth nearly shat herself," Gordon says. He keeps his voice down because Ruth and Wendy are upstairs, getting ready. "She hasn't been outside since."

Martin walks over to the window and looks out. Gordon had wiped down the table and mopped up Ruth's spilled coffee, but her unfinished croissant is still sitting there in the late evening sun.

"Thing with frogs," Martin says, "is that they're creatures of habit, they like to take the same path from A to B every single time, like it's passed down to them. Like it's in their DNA, you know. Same path, every time." He turns back to Gordon and raises his bottle of beer.

"Don't tell Ruth," Gordon says. "She'll be packing her bags and moving back to London." He takes a long swig of beer. He's had a few already, probably too many. "I thought that was elephants?" he says, wiping his mouth with the back of his hand.

"What?"

"Elephants. I thought elephants did that, you know, using the same paths to the watering holes and all that."

Martin thinks about it and says, "No, definitely frogs."

*

Gordon dreams about frogs and elephants, about frogs as big as elephants, stampeding over the patio, trampling the table and chairs and flattening the weeds and thistles.

Wendy is lying next to him, snoring. It's their first time for a while, the first time in the new house, and Gordon thinks it didn't go too well. Probably his fault. Maybe it was the beer. Or maybe Wendy was just tired after the long drive up.

Ruth and Martin don't seem to be having any problems. Still going at it. Gordon lies awake, smiling to himself. He thinks about waking Wendy and having another go, but he lets her sleep. He knows she'll be good again in the morning and ready for more, all in her own good time.

He gets up and tiptoes along the landing, stepping over the loose floorboard near the door.

Ruth's on top, her back arched, her hair in Martin's face.

"Sorry," Gordon says, climbing in beside them. Ruth reaches out to him, gives him a gentle stroke and says, "Nearly done, love."

"Take your time," Gordon says. He sits up on his elbow to get a better look.

Martin smiles and gives him the thumbs up.

Gordon can't wait for them to finish so he can tell them about his dream, about the frogs as big as elephants.

Monkey Blood

Jack and Grace waited on the bench as Megan skipped off towards the ice cream van. They'd given her a handful of change: tens and twenties and some of the coppers they'd been putting aside for the weekend. Not much, but enough for a large 99.

"Make sure you get a Flake with it," Grace said. They'd charged her for a 99 last time and tried to diddle her out of the Flake.

"And don't forget the nuts," Jack said. "And the sauce. Just say yes if the bloke says do you want some sauce. Some of that raspberry sauce, the monkey blood."

He sat back, arms outstretched, and looked up at the sun.

"She'll drop it," he said, feeling his eyes burn. "How much do you want to bet?"

Grace had her camera out, zooming in on Megan and then panning out to take in the castle and the dunes.

"Just you wait and see," Jack said. "The minute the guy hands her the ice cream she'll drop it all over the fucking place."

Grace had warned him earlier, in the car. Said she'd give him a right good clip if he didn't stop. All you ever do, she'd said, always having a fucking pop at her, the poor thing. Jack had let it go. It was the weekend and he was looking forward to plodging around in the rock pools. He didn't want a fight, not at the seaside.

He wondered though, about Megan. He didn't know if it was just a phase she was going through or if they were all like that at that age. Dropping things, bumping into things, tripping over things. All gorm-less, all feet and elbows.

"Maybe we should get her looked at," Jack said, blinking, rubbing his eyes. "You know, just to make sure she's okay."

In the Event of a Zombie Apocalypse

The beans had been on sale: fifteen pence a tin. They weren't Heinz, but still. He bought ninety-six tins and lugged them down into the cellar. Stacked them in the corner, next to his composting toilet and assorted machetes. Then he barricaded himself in and waited. He'd give it a month, maybe six weeks. Wait till the worst was over, then come out, blades swinging. He had a hammer too, tucked into the waistband of his combats, just in case. Then he'd show them who was crazy.

Sophie

Your mother ushers you into the kitchen and says not to worry, she'll make you a strong cup of tea. Says she'll get you some biscuits too while she's at it, your favourites.

"Your dad's out back," she says. "In the shed."

You step outside. Can hear him hammering away at the bottom of the garden. You knock on the shed door and go in.

"Christ," he says, not looking up, "you're back again?"

You used to have your own little corner of the shed when you were a kid, when your dad and your granda thought you might be interested in hammering things, in fixing things and making things. Your dad set up a little workbench for you, said you could use his tools, his real tools.

There's a deckchair in the corner now: red, green and yellow stripes, all faded, sun-bleached. Last time you sat in it you came out in a rash: big yellow pus-filled spots all over your backside.

"What happened this time?" your dad asks.

You pick up a tool from the bench. It's got a wooden handle and a pointy metal end. You have no idea what it is or what you're supposed to do with it.

Your dad used to joke with you, used to say,

"Scott, get me that sliding bevel, will you? And while you're at it, Scottie, do us a favour and pass me the spokeshave."

You feel the weight of the metal thing in your hand, and tell him what happened with Meg.

He listens, stops hammering. Gives you that look.

"She was *too nice?*" he says.

You nod.

"You need to get your bloody head seen to." He starts hammering again. "You're forty-four, man. You need to settle down."

"I'm forty-two."

He stops hammering again, but only for a second.

"What about that other girl?" he asks. "Claudia?"

You haven't seen Claudia for months. You weren't with her very long: a week or two.

"Oh yes," your dad says. "I remember now. She bit her fingernails. You told her to sling her hook because she bit her fingernails."

The tool's heavier than it looks, and the pointy end scares you a little bit, so you put it back down before you hurt yourself.

"She never stopped," you say. "It was disgusting. She'd have a mouthful of food and she'd still be chewing away on those nails. Disgusting."

Your dad shakes his head.

You think he's going to launch into his usual spiel: he'll bring up a name and remind you why you dumped them. Tessa: her teeth. Helen: she smelled. Liz: only one leg. Lots of others, some you remember, some you don't.

You wonder how he manages to remember them

all. You think he must take notes. A little black book. Your little black book of shame.

He puts the hammer down and picks up a bigger hammer.

"You should have stayed with Sophie," he says. He nods. Your dad liked Sophie, a lot. He holds the hammer up to the light and examines the heavy end. The end you hit things with.

"She was too French," you say.

He gives you that look again.

"She was *Italian*."

You shrug. You're fairly certain she was French. "French, Italian, it doesn't matter."

The Fourth Wife

Holly hears him downstairs in the kitchen, tripping over something, dropping something, kicking something. When it goes quiet, she rolls over, her back to the door, and tries to sleep.

She used to worry when she couldn't hear anything. That he'd fallen, hurt himself. That she'd find him dead on the kitchen floor the next morning, cold as the grey granite tiles, his head cracked wide open.

She doesn't worry now. She hears him mumbling, the kitchen door closing, the footsteps in the dining room. She hears the rattling of keys as he unlocks his office door, then nothing again.

He keeps a photo of his first wife in the bottom drawer of his filing cabinet. He hides the key for the filing cabinet on the middle row of his bookshelf, halfway along, behind a copy of *Ulysses*. He once told her that was his favourite book, but she suspects he's never read it.

Sometimes Holly sneaks downstairs, long after it's gone quiet, and tiptoes her way into the dining room. She peeks through his office window and sees him on the sofa or slumped over his desk. Sometimes the crumpled photo of his first wife is still in his hand. Sometimes it's on the floor, next to the empty bottle.

*

She must have nodded off. She hears him coming up the stairs, stopping on the landing, breathing heavily. She closes her eyes and pretends she's sleeping. Sometimes that's enough to put him off, but not tonight. He grunts, kicks his shoes under the bed and climbs in next to her. He reaches for her with one of his huge meaty hands, and rolls on top of her.

Holly never knew his first wife, but sometimes she meets up with wives two and three. She doesn't say anything, nothing specific, but she doesn't have to. Wife Two says Holly can stay with her, for as long as she wants. She's got a spare room, it's not much, but Holly can have it. Holly says she'll think about it. She thinks about it now as he whispers her name into the pillow and says he's sorry.

The Little Things

It was the little things that started to get to him. The way she held her fork. That thing she did with her hair, pulling it all the way back like that. Her snoring. Her *face*.

He'd never had a problem with her face before. He'd wondered about it, about when her face first started to annoy him, but he couldn't pinpoint the exact moment. There had to be a point, a specific point when something changed: when he went from liking her face to not liking her face. Or maybe it was a gradual process, something that had seeped into the marriage over the years, bit by bit, unnoticed till it was fully formed.

Whatever it was, he knew he used to like her face (he used to like her face very much) but now he didn't.

He told her the next morning, halfway through the scrambled eggs. Choosing his words carefully, he said, "I've got to be honest, Trish, your face is really beginning to bother me."

She stopped, the fork halfway to her mouth, balanced between thumb and index finger. That still bothered him, but not as much as it used to, not since he'd started having a problem with her face.

"What's wrong with it?" Trish asked. "With my face?"

"I don't know. It's just ... I don't know."

Trish got up and poured some more coffee.

"Are you okay?" he asked, waiting till she was sitting down again, the coffee pot out of harm's way. "I mean, I—"

"It's okay," she said.

"It is?"

"It is if you still love me. You do, don't you?"

They'd been together for so long he hadn't really thought about it for a while. So he thought about it now, and quickly came to the conclusion that, yes, he still loved her.

"I do," he said. "A lot."

"That's okay, then."

"It is?"

She was smiling.

"What?"

"My mother used to say looks aren't that important, not really."

It was just the kind of thing her mother would say. Trish's mother could be brutally honest, even with her own daughter.

"Look," he said. He reached out and took her hand, almost wishing he hadn't said anything now. "Your mother, she—"

"Oh, I know," Trish said. "It's fine, though. She was talking about you, not me."

Uncle Colin

Uncle Colin died while we were having pudding. Not a squeak, just toppled forward, face first into his plum crumble.

"I think Uncle Colin just died," I said.

Mum and Dad looked at Uncle Colin, then at each other.

I got up and had a closer look.

"Maybe he's just sleeping," I said. I felt for a pulse and prodded him.

"Definitely dead," I said and sat back down.

"Maybe they were off," Dad said. "The plums."

"I don't think so," Mum said. "I only just bought them yesterday. On sale, buy one, get one free."

Dad got up and poured himself another coffee from the pot. "We should probably do something with him," he said.

Mum nodded. Uncle Colin was her brother and they'd been close once, but that was a long time ago.

"Maybe he was allergic," Dad said. "To plums."

"Can you be allergic to plums?" Mum asked.

Dad shrugged.

"Maybe it was his ticker," I said. "How old was he, Mum?"

Mum thought about it for a bit. "Fifty-eight, I think. Or fifty-nine. Something like that."

We buried him in the back garden, next to the cabbages.

"You sure he was dead?" Mum asked later, settling down for the late news.

"Yes, I'm pretty sure," I said.

I got up. Looked out the window into the darkness. "If he wasn't, I reckon he is now."

Unfinished Business

She'd propped herself up with a few pillows, the duvet over her legs. She was smoking, even though he'd asked her not to, not in the bedroom. She was using the glass from the bedside table, the one he used for his teeth, as a makeshift ashtray. She watched him come back into the room, the towel around his waist. "I like your belly," she said, kicking the duvet away and uncrossing her legs. He stopped and looked down. Breathed in. "What belly?" He could have said the same about her. Could have said much worse, but he didn't. He didn't want her to leave, not yet.

While She Sleeps

He looks at the clock on the bedside table. 11:57. She likes to go to bed early, around nine o'clock: usually in a deep sleep by now, locked down, switched off, like someone pulled a plug on her. But something's not right tonight. She's restless, her eyelids flickering.

Maybe she knows. That's his first thought. Knows that he likes to watch her, that he watches her every night. Hours on end, sometimes, ever since they first met.

She rolls over, towards the wall, then back again, towards him, pushing the blankets down around her waist. She's wearing an old T-shirt, a few sizes too big for her, scrunched up around her middle. She works out and it shows: the tight stomach, the sinewy arms.

He smiles. It's his little secret: much as he loves her, and he really does love her, there are some things she doesn't need to know.

They met in the supermarket, in the frozen vegetable aisle. She smiled. Didn't say anything, but didn't have to. That smile, that was enough for him.

She settles, finally. Her breathing's slower. Sometimes, when she's out for good, when she's in that place she goes to, it's like she's not even breathing at all, and he has to get as close as he can without waking her, without startling her, to make sure she's all right.

He doesn't know what he'd do if something happened to her. Maybe that's why he watches her, why he never takes his eyes off her.

She mumbles something. She often does that, jabbering away to herself, sometimes about work, sometimes about friends, sometimes about nothing at all: just words, gibberish.

He can't make out what she's saying so he leans forward, his weight on his elbow. A bit closer. Close as he can get, till his ear's pressed up hard against the cold window.

He tries to get a better view by holding on to the sill, but the ladder wobbles and he stops and steadies himself.

He's never been good with heights and it's a long way down to the patio.

The Island

They found a crumbling farmhouse on top of the hill, just outside the village. A good spot, on high ground, three miles from the coast. Close enough to see the sea; to see the island.

Charlie and Callie were upstairs in the main bedroom, watching. They'd lost four people the night before: four good people. The others had wanted to head inland, into the hills, but Charlie said the island would be safer. They'd have boats and they could fish and go ashore for supplies. They'd go in teams, armed and ready, and take whatever they needed. In and out, no messing about.

"They'd still be alive," Charlie said. "They shouldn't have listened to me." He'd carved his name into the old oak dresser next to the window, and was picking at it with his hunting knife.

"They'd have frozen up there," Callie said. "Two days in the hills and they'd all be dead."

Callie looked out over the fields, towards the island. She wanted a hot bath and clean sheets and breakfast in bed. She wanted Chris and Alex and Robyn, the way it used to be.

"How's everyone?" Charlie asked, turning to face her.

Callie shrugged. "The girls are sleeping. Tom's

watching over them. Cath and Paul are out back. Cath found a couple of hunting rifles in the cellar."

"Daniel?"

Daniel had lost his wife and son the night before. Daniel's son had been the same age as her Alex.

Callie shook her head. Eventually she said, "Connor says there's a farm on the island, so there'll be tractors and equipment, plenty of food and fuel, enough to keep us going. There's cattle and pigs, and we can—"

She stopped and smiled. It was the first time Charlie had seen her smile for a long time.

"What?" he asked.

"I was going to say we can live off the land, the fat of the land. And have rabbits, you know, like George and Lennie."

Charlie looked blankly at her.

"*Of Mice and Men.* George and Lennie, the two main characters, they have this thing, this dream. They're going to buy some land, just the two of them, and grow their own vegetables and keep rabbits and chickens and—"

"I've never read it," Charlie said, turning back to the window.

They were quiet for a while and then Charlie said, "Is it a happy ending? The story?"

"No," Callie said quietly, "it's not."

Escapology

It wasn't till the next morning that they realised the pig was missing.

The pig had been Diane's idea. Joe had wanted a goldfish, low-maintenance, but she'd dug her heels in. Got what she wanted, as per usual.

Diane had popped out with the leftover crusts and a mouldy apple. Joe was in the kitchen, having another coffee, when he heard her scream. She'd not been well for a while, what with her leg and everything, and an image flashed in front of him. Diane, face down in the mud.

He found her outside the shed. Crying but still very much alive.

"Look," she sobbed, pointing.

The shed door was open. Joe's makeshift lock was on the ground, splintered. Diane had said they should have bought a proper padlock, just to be on the safe side. Joe had said it'd be fine, it was a fucking pig, not Harry fucking Houdini.

Joe poked his head round the door. Pig shit and pig piss all over the linoleum floor, but no pig.

"Fuck," he said, getting down on one knee. He picked up a piece of pig shit and rubbed it between his thumb and forefinger. He smelled it.

"It's okay," he said. "It's fresh. He can't have gone far."

Calm

She goes in through the side gate.

It's dark but she knows exactly where to go: up the path, round the side of the house, over the patio. She knows they like to keep the conservatory door open till late, and knows the husband is away on a business trip to Hong Kong and won't be back till tomorrow night. She slides the door open another few inches, just enough to squeeze through.

The mother's in the living room, asleep on the sofa. She stops, looks down at her. She's even prettier up close. She knows she shouldn't but she reaches out and touches her, runs her fingers through her soft hair. She leans forward and kisses her on the lips, and whispers a silent thank you before making for the stairs.

The first room on the right: this was always going to be the trickiest part, but she's calm, calmer than she ever imagined. It will probably hit her later, back in the safety of her own home, but for now she doesn't even hesitate, removes her padded rucksack and just gets on with it, exactly as she'd planned. She leaves the way she came, out through the back and into the darkness.

She doesn't have far to walk, which is good because he's a lot heavier than she expected.

Employee of the Month

Steve, friend of a friend, was sitting behind his desk in a cheap suit.

"Look," he said, "I'm not being funny, but a fucking monkey could do this job. It's yours if you want it."

"You haven't seen my CV," Eddie said.

"Do you have one?"

"No."

Steve shrugged. The suit was too small, the elbows shiny, nearly worn through. "You want it or not?"

Eddie said okay, he might as well take it, see how things go.

"This way," Steve said, getting up.

Eddie followed him out of the office and on to the factory floor.

"Watch," Steve said, pulling up a swivel chair at the conveyor belt. Eddie watched as Steve picked up a metal part from the belt and put it into a cardboard box next to his chair. Steve did it again, and again. Three metal parts into the cardboard box. Then he turned to Eddie.

"That's it?" Eddie said.

"That's it." Steve got up. Tried to smooth down the creases in his trousers. "Any questions?"

Eddie thought about it and said no.

"Do you even know what we do here?" Steve asked. "What we make?" He took one of the metal parts from the box and turned it over in his hand. It was about the size of a matchbox, an inch thick, with a hole drilled right through the middle.

Eddie looked around, at the conveyor belt, at the metal part, at the other workers on the line.

"No idea," he said. He'd asked his friend about it but all he'd said was metal parts and shit, and Eddie had left it at that.

Steve nodded, like he was pleased he didn't have to explain anything.

"You'll be fine," he said. "Just don't fuck anything up."

He left Eddie to it. By lunchtime Eddie had a headache. He was hungry, too, so he followed everyone into the canteen and piled his plate high with mince and potatoes and gravy.

He sat by himself in the corner and watched everyone else eating and talking, and he thought this is what it must be like, to work for a living.

"First day?"

He looked up, his mouth full. He recognised her from the factory floor: the quiet girl with the straggly hair who hadn't said a word to anyone all morning.

"How'd you guess?"

Eddie budged along, making room for her, even though it was just him on a table for six.

"Have a seat," he said.

"I never sit down at lunchtime."

"Why not?"

"I don't know."

She brushed a straggle of hair from her face and looked down at his plate. "How is it?"

"Watery spuds, stringy mince. I wouldn't feed my dog this shit."

"You have a dog?"

"No. If I did, though."

He shovelled up another forkful — a hot meal was a hot meal — and said, "How long you been here?"

"Eight years."

"*Eight years?* Fucking hell."

He'd watched her earlier, her hands a blur as she grabbed, packed, grabbed, packed, like she could do it in her sleep.

"What are you," Eddie said, "Employee of the Month or something?"

She shrugged. Almost smiled.

She took a squashed packet of cigarettes from her back pocket and said, "Do you want one?"

Eddie checked his watch and said, "I can't. I'm leaving. Soon as I've finished this."

"Leaving?"

"I'm quitting."

"You only just started."

He looked around. "It's not for me. All this. Work."

She nodded. "What will you do?"

"Something else." Eddie shrugged.

"Like what?"

"Something. Anything. I'll have a think. Take it easy for a bit, and see what comes up."

He polished off the last of the potatoes and would have licked the plate clean if he'd been on his own.

"You should quit," he said, wiping his mouth with the back of his sleeve.

"I can't."

"Why not?"

"I don't know."

"Eight years? You should definitely quit."

He got up. "Well?"

"Well what?"

"Are you coming?"

She brushed the hair from her face again.

"I don't know," she said, following him out.

Number 27

Doug watches them through the gap in the curtains. He's dimmed the living room lights to get a better look. Two removal vans and a couple of four-by-fours. Less than an hour and they're all in. Mother, father, two kids, grandmother, cat.

Indians, he thinks.

*

"That lot at Number 27," Graeme says. "Syrians, apparently. Refugees." He thinks about it. "Or maybe Iraqis. Something like that."

*

The landing's a tad cramped, but it gives Doug a much better view of the house. He sets up a little table, the foldy one that used to be in the conservatory, and has a good hunt in the shed for a chair. He finds one eventually: green, plastic, with a wonky leg, so not ideal, not with his back, but it will do for now. He'll be fine, and he's got his flask, and some biscuits.

*

"Definitely Syrians," Graeme says.

He says everyone was talking about it in the Bell the other night and the general consensus is that they're Syrians.

*

Doug has another rummage, under the stairs this

time, and finds an extension cable for the phone. Much better, as he can now watch the new arrivals at 27 and report back to Graeme at the same time. A running commentary, without having to traipse up and down the stairs every five minutes.

He found some binoculars too, and he thinks they're going to come in very handy.

*

Doug's fairly sure they're not Syrians.

He was minding his own business behind the bushes at the bottom of the garden and he couldn't help hearing them, on the other side of the road, whispering. All very hush-hush, all very conspiratorial. He's not exactly sure what Indian sounds like, but it sounded like Indian to him.

Later, from the landing, he was watching the two young ones, the little boy and girl, playing cricket round the side of the house. There's a yard out there, part paving, part gravel, and they were using one of the rubbish bins, the blue recycling bin, for stumps. Doug couldn't believe it. That little girl. What an arm on her. He called Graeme and ended up giving him a ball-by-ball commentary, like it was *Test Match Special* or something. Doug said he was *very* impressed with the girl, with her run-up and delivery, the way she made that ball turn.

Graeme doesn't seem convinced though, despite her cricketing prowess, and thinks they still might be Syrians.

"What about the boy?" he asks.

Doug watches the boy swing and miss, almost knocking himself off his feet.

"The boy's hopeless," Doug says. "Bloody hopeless."

*

Doug comes to the conclusion that the mother is a fine-looking woman when you see her up-close. He thinks he probably wouldn't have given her a second look if he'd met her on the street or on the bus, but up-close, with the binoculars, there's no getting away from it. She's an incredibly beautiful woman. Lovely teeth.

*

Graeme says they were talking about it in the pub again. Says he did a straw poll in the downstairs bar. Seven against two. Definitely Syrians. Not just Syrians, but refugees. Or migrants, he says, whatever you want to call them.

*

Graeme's given up on his vantage point at the top of his stairs. Says he has a much better view of the back of the house if he climbs up into the loft and stands on his tiptoes.

He says it'll be good to keep a closer eye on them. Says he's bought a notebook, like Doug, to record their various comings and goings. So far, he says, he hasn't seen anything of interest at all. Except the cat, which was sleeping on the patio.

*

Doug buys one of those snuggle blankets, for the cold nights on the landing. He's thinking of investing in a new chair too, preferably one that's not plastic and wonky-legged. An armchair, ideally. But he's not sure how he'd get it up the stairs. Graeme says he'll help, but they both know Graeme's knees aren't what they used to be.

It occurs to Doug that he hasn't seen the dad for a few days.

"You ask me," he says to Graeme, "that dad's a bit of a funny one."

Graeme says, "Oh?"

"Leaves first thing in the morning, doesn't come back till God knows when," Doug says. "Like I said, very funny, and I don't mean funny ha-ha, if you know what I mean."

He takes out his notebook and has to flip back three or four pages for the last sighting of the dad. Midnight, Tuesday. Doug clears his throat and reads out his notes and observations: "Dad returns. Yawning. Looks like he hasn't slept for a week. Looks like he's up to something."

"Hmm," Graeme says.

"Exactly," Doug says.

*

Graeme says he saw the grandmother in the post office. Buying stamps. Says he was just standing there on the other side of the partition, pretending he was browsing through the birthday cards, and she looked right at him and smiled. Just like that, for no reason. Smiled right at him and said hello on her way out.

*

"I mean, it's not on, is it?" Doug says. It's late, and he pours himself another cup of tea from the flask. He's out of biscuits, even the soggy Rich Teas he'd left till last.

Graeme says he's going to put an extra shift in, mid-morning to lunchtime. "About time we ratcheted things up a bit," he says. The knees are still giving him gyp, he says, but he found an old wooden crate in the loft and now he doesn't have to stretch quite so much to see through the skylight.

Doug suggests daily briefings so that they can cross-reference each other's notes and share intelligence. "Knowledge," he says, suddenly feeling all-knowing, "that's what it's all about, because knowledge is power."

Graeme agrees and starts by running through the previous day's movements. He says he saw the little ones, the boy and girl, heading off to school with the mother at 8:44 and then—

Doug listens to the shuffling of paper, to Graeme exhaling.

"Is that it?" Doug asks.

Graeme checks his notes again. "That's it," he says. "Except the cat. I saw the cat again. It had a massive shit on the patio."

*

Doug raises the issue with the woman from the parish council. He's on the landing, with the binoculars, the phone on hands-free. The dad's home. The dad has been home all day, playing with the kids, lying on the sofa and watching TV. Cooking in the kitchen.

Doug tells her about the comings and goings, the early starts and late nights, everything.

"No," the woman from the council says when he's finished. "It's just not on."

Doug nods furiously to himself. The woman from the council is a formidable little woman. An ally. He doesn't care that no one likes her, her and her clipboard.

"And the smell!" she says. "That *smell*."

Doug doesn't know what to say, so he says nothing.

"Curry and such things," the woman from the council says, clicking her tongue. "That smell, wafting all over the village like that."

*

Doug puts the binoculars down. He rubs his eyes and watches the house. The lights are on in the living room but the curtains are drawn. All quiet. Nothing happening.

He thinks about the woman from the council. The smell doesn't bother him one little bit. Sometimes, and he's never mentioned this to Graeme, he'll find himself opening a window, despite the cold, so he can breathe it in.

He looks around, at the binoculars and the note-pads and the pencils he sharpens every day and keeps in an old jam jar on the table. He said he'd call Graeme later, to debrief him on his meeting. But he thinks that can wait.

Terms and Conditions

Tania stood next to the bed and looked down at him. She smiled: the way he was lying, dead to the world, his arms and legs splayed out like that, he looked like a starfish.

She reached forward and traced a finger over his stomach, round and round, down, all the way down. Watched him twitch and spring back to life — even now, after everything she'd done to him.

She tiptoed out of the bedroom, not wanting to wake him. He'd need his rest. He'd need all the rest he could get because she wasn't finished with him yet.

*

She met Georgie in the bar half an hour before their shift started. First thing Georgie said was, "So?"

Tania shrugged. She watched Georgie light up: watched her close her eyes, her eyelashes fluttering, as she inhaled. Tania could have killed for a smoke, for one puff, but she looked away and took in the bar, the spilled beer, the crusty tables, the cracked windows. Immediately wished she hadn't because all it did was remind her that she was stuck here for the next eight hours, doing a shitty job for shitty money, when he was there, in her bed, waiting for her.

Georgie leaned forward, elbows on the table, and whispered.

"How was it?"

She turned her head to the side and exhaled slowly, towards the No Smoking sign on the wall. Shitty job, shitty bar, but there were some staff perks.

Tania shook her head.

The guy had come on to Georgie first, like they all did. Tania was fine with that. You had a friend like Georgie, you had to be fine with that, because they all hit on Georgie first, all the time. Like they were wired that way, like it was in their DNA.

"Nothing happened," Tania said. "He said he'd walk me home, and we're not even halfway there and he stops, just like that, and throws up, all over the place." She shrugged again. "He headed back this way, said he was going home."

Georgie relaxed and sat back. "Prick," she said. "I told you he was trouble."

The guy *was* a prick. A total prick. Hitting on Georgie, then the others, one by one, before turning to Tania late on, when the place had thinned out and they were getting ready to lock up. Tania had brought him a glass of water from the bar, told him it was on the house. He grabbed her wrist and pulled her in close. He wasn't much to look at, all angles and sharp edges, and Tania must have had a good fifty pounds on him, but he squeezed so hard she thought he might snap her wrist in two. Would have, if she hadn't reached down with her free hand and undid his zip. I only live around the corner, she whispered in his ear. If you want to, you know, walk me home.

"You're probably right," Tania said. "Big time prick."

"Trust me," Georgie said, blowing smoke across the table. "I know trouble when I see it."

*

Tania found him exactly as she'd left him, as if she'd never been away. But he was awake now, and he'd shat himself. Sooner or later, they all shat themselves. It used to bother her, but not now. It was just one of those things: an inevitable consequence, an occupational hazard.

She'd cuffed his wrists and ankles, shackled him to the four corners of the bed, starfish-like. He heard her before he saw her, the squeaky floorboards announcing her arrival. His head shot up off the mattress when she walked over to the bed, his neck muscles straining, his eyes bulging, screaming out for help.

She did what she always did, and ignored him. She'd found that was the best course of action when they were like that, when they were a little overexcited. Ignore them. Sometimes that set them off even more, and she'd stand there and smile, sometimes laugh at them, her arms folded over her chest.

This one had surprised her. For a skinny little runt he'd put up a pretty good fight when she'd cuffed him, thrashing around like he was having a fit, trying to chew her hand off when she stuffed the socks into his mouth and reached for the heavy-duty tape she kept in the top drawer of her bedside table.

She'd had to use all her weight against him, grinding her big backside down against his chest, digging her knees into his scrawny biceps. She hit him in the face a couple of times too, to calm him down, short, sharp jabs, and kept hitting him till he stopped

81

thrashing — till his body went limp and the muffled screams subsided and all he could do was bleat like a pathetic, wounded animal.

She almost pitied him, looking down at him now. Almost.

She reached for the table again, the bottom drawer this time, and took out the camcorder.

"We need to talk," she said, pressing the record button and pointing the camcorder at his face, a close-up, before zooming out slowly. "We need to talk about terms and conditions."

Shelter

"Me and you," he says, winking.

Becky looks over towards the bar, at the woman reading yesterday's paper, at the old guy in the corner picking his nose. She reaches for her drink. She's had a few: four or five, maybe more.

"You and I," she says, over the rim of her glass. His name is Robert. That's what he'd said: *Robert, but you can call me Bob*.

"You what?" he says.

"It should be *you and I*. Technically, I mean. Grammatically."

Robert clears his throat. He's phlegmy, blocked up. Becky watches him swallow, can almost hear it go down.

They told her to get out more, to make an effort. To move on. But she doesn't think this is what they had in mind for her.

Throat cleared, Robert gets up and sits down next to her, against the wall.

"What are you doing?" Becky says. She doesn't budge. Doesn't want to give her ground. Robert has been eating crisps. Cheese and onion. She can smell them on his breath, mixed with beer and cigarettes. But there's something else, in his hair, in his grey, straggly beard: something damp, earthy.

He offers his hand. "I'm Robert," he says, "but—"

Becky cuts him off. "You already said that, when you first came over here. You're repeating yourself, Robert. Sorry, *Robert but you can call me Bob*."

She takes his hand. It's warm, his fingers thick and calloused.

*

"Got myself a little place not far from here," he says. He crosses his legs, his mud-caked boot brushing against her knee. "How about we head out there and, you know."

"Don't do that," Becky says.

"What?"

"That winking thing."

"Was I winking?"

Becky nods. "It's very off-putting."

"It works, you know. Sometimes."

Becky empties the last few drops of her drink and then helps herself to his lukewarm beer.

"Where is it?" she asks. "This place of yours." She wipes her mouth with the back of her sleeve. She doesn't usually drink beer, but then she doesn't usually sit in pubs like this talking to people like him.

"Not far. Out in the woods."

"Which woods?"

"Just the woods. Built the place myself. A little hideaway, just in case."

"In case what?"

"You know, in case everything goes tits up."

Becky raises his glass. "I'll drink to that," she says and spills some of it down the front of her jacket.

Robert offers her a crumpled tissue from his inside

84

pocket and says, "You know, I can gut a deer in less than eight minutes."

Becky puts her hand on his knee. His camouflaged trousers are almost worn right through. His knee is cold, razor-sharp.

"Eight minutes," he says, grinning. "Them deer, they're everywhere up there. Deer, rabbits, squirrels. *Badgers*. Trust me, when it all goes to shit *I'll* not be hungry."

He puts his hand on top of hers, and winks.

"My van's out back," he says.

Odd Socks

"You'll have to wash it first," she says.

She's never asked him to wash it before. She looks up from her book and peers at him, her glasses perched on the end of her fat nose.

He gives it a good scrub in the bathroom, with soap and warm water, and dries it off with one of her flannels. He sprinkles some talcum powder on it, then wipes it off.

He stands next to the bed.

"Clean?" she says, not looking up.

"As a whistle."

She turns the page, her lips moving as she reads. Sometimes, when he listens carefully, he can hear her mouthing the words. He used to find this endearing, one of her many little idiosyncrasies.

He waits by the side of the bed. He doesn't know what to do with his hands. She smiles to herself, like she's forgotten he's there, and turns another page.

He looks down. He's still wearing his socks. Odd ones: one white, one grey. There's a hole in the white one, revealing a long yellow toenail. He's surprised she hasn't said anything about it, about the socks. She used to refuse point-blank to do it while he still had his socks on, odd or even, with or without holes, as if that would be breaking some unwritten rule or crossing some invisible line. Now, she doesn't seem to mind.

The Streets

The routine helps, a bit. He thinks.

He explains this to the counsellor, after he's explained why Julie can't make it to the meeting. The counsellor nods, sympathetically. That way she nods, her head tilted ever so slightly to one side, towards her left shoulder. That's good, she says, meaning the routine, not the fact that Julie has missed yet another appointment. The counsellor's eyes are wet, and he thinks this is all well and good, sharing the pain and everything, but then he thinks, hang on a fucking minute, *I'm* the one who's supposed to be crying, not you. *Me*. Not you.

*

He puts on his walking boots and his big blue overcoat. He grabs the scarf Julie bought him last Christmas, and his woolly hat. No gloves though. He owns at least a dozen pairs of gloves, but he never wears them. Keeps them in a drawer in the hallway, just in case. In case of what, he's not sure.

It's the same every night, his little routine. Along William's Way, then Crag Street, then Burnside, then Westland Road. His hands cold, crying out for a nice pair of warm gloves. Along Dinningside, into Kew Drive, hands buried deep into his pockets, fingers grabbing the fleecy lining for warmth.

*

There's no one else out. Not on a night like this, cold enough to take your face off.

The counsellor suggested he buy a dog. After she wiped her eyes and stopped crying, she said it might be good. A dog. A companion for you, she said, for your night-time walks.

He said he didn't like dogs, never had done and probably never would. The counsellor smiled and nodded again, her eyes welling up.

*

He takes a shortcut when he gets to Bell Road, up the narrow path between the pebble-dashed houses. It's a steep climb, and dark, what little light there is blocked out by the overhanging thorn bushes.

He looks down, has to watch his step. Dog shit everywhere. But he doesn't mind, not really. Thinks if he ever took the counsellor's advice and bought a dog, an Alsatian or a Rottweiler, something big and mean, then he'd probably let it shit on the path too.

*

He's worried about Julie.

He thinks she's not coping, not at all. He thinks she hasn't even begun to cope.

*

He stops at the shop on the corner and buys some milk. Some cigarettes too. He's smoking again. It helps, like the routine. It was just the odd one, a few here and there to begin with, but he's on a packet a day now. The counsellor asked him about the smoking, and he shrugged. What's the worst that could happen, he said, and anyway, it helps.

The old woman behind the counter makes small talk, as she does every night, but she never mentions the baby. Like the baby never existed, like they never had it and never lost it.

She stares out of the window, into the black, and says it looks like they're in for a cold one this time, maybe even some snow. A proper winter, she says, handing him his change.

*

He told Julie he'd not be long, half an hour or so.

She'll be in bed now, her pills on the table. He's not sure about the pills. The drink, too. The counsellor nodded sympathetically when he told her about the pills and the drink, and scribbled some notes in her notepad and said they should talk about it next time, with Julie, if she could make it.

*

He retraces his steps, through the cut, dodging the dog shit, ducking his head to avoid the overhanging thorns, up Bell Road and Kew Drive and Dinningside. Along Westland Road, Burnside, Crag Street, William's Way, till he's home, outside, the house in darkness.

He stands at the gate and tries to remember what it was like before, before they lost everything.

He reaches for the gate, but turns and walks away from the house.

Back along William's Way.

The routine, he reminds himself. It's all about the routine.

Fish Heads

Pete pokes his head through the filthy curtains and looks out on to the backyard.

"There's a guy out there decapitating fish," he says. "With a machete."

Mona's examining the damp patch on the wall, near the door.

"I think it's coming in through the gutter," she says, ignoring him. She reaches up and touches it with the tip of her rubber-gloved finger. "It's soaking wet," she says. "I thought they were fixing that?"

Pete's not bothered about the damp patch. He's more concerned about the smell from the fish and chip shop next door. Mona says they'll get used to it. It'll be fine, she says, as long as they keep the windows shut and buy a fan or something to keep the air circulating, like the estate agent said.

"Fucking place," Pete says, turning and looking around. That smell, the fish and chips, the grease, the fat, was part of him now, like a second skin.

They'd done this together, he thinks, the pair of them. They both signed the papers, they both knew what they were doing. But he still feels responsible. He still feels he's let her down.

"A lick of paint," Mona says, stepping away from the wall.

Pete looks down at the stained carpet, at the ancient gas fire, at the criss-cross of slug trails near the air vent.

"A good lick of paint and it'll be fine," Mona says.

Pete turns his back on her, back towards the window. She's never seen him cry before.

She comes up behind him and wraps her arms around his waist. Pete peers through the curtains. The guy in the white overalls is tossing the fish heads into a big plastic bucket. Pete wonders what they do with them, with all the fish heads: if there's a market for them, or if they just chuck them out with the other rubbish. Maybe they have a special licence or something, to get rid of them.

"You can't just toss them into the bin," he says.

"What?"

"The fish heads. The stinking fucking fish heads."

"Come on," Mona says, letting go.

"You can't," he says, not moving. "You can't just stick them in the bin."

How Not to Make an Exit

He lights the wrong end of his cigarette, and bristles when she points it out to him. He thought he was having one of his better days.

"Maybe I prefer it that way," he says, getting up off the bed and storming out.

He slams the door behind him and thinks, That'll fucking teach her.

She waits on the bed, counting the minutes till he re-emerges from the wardrobe.

Rapeseed

Hannah comes prepared: long summer dress and no knickers. Don's already there, in his new jogging gear, the flu mask he bought off the Internet tucked into the elasticated waistband of his too-tight shorts.

Hannah smiles and takes his hand and leads him deeper into the sea of yellow. He wonders how many others have been before him, how many other hands. But he thinks it best not to dwell on the details. It's easier that way.

Paula had sneered when he said he was popping out for a run. "A *run?*" she'd said, studying him over the rim of her glasses. He'd looked down, over the swell of his belly, at the toes of his shiny new trainers. "Since when have you *popped out for a run?*" She'd snorted before turning back to her newspaper.

"We could have just gone to a hotel," Don says to Hannah. He knows what he is doing is wrong, but he's never felt more right about anything in his life. "You know," he says, "*inside.* Out of harm's way." He flaps at the invisible germs with his free hand and tries not to gag on the sickly sweet air that clings to him like a wet towel.

It started with a twitch last time, his first time with Hannah. Then a sneeze. Hannah opened her eyes, looked up at him, her heel in the small of his back, keeping him exactly where she wanted him. "It's okay," he'd said, slowing down but not stopping, "it's just this fucking rapeseed, it fucking—"

He sneezed again, four or five times, till his nose bled, the blood mixing with the hot tears cascading down his face.

"I know a place," he says. "Nice and discreet. They have these four-poster beds and—"

Hannah pulls her hand free and starts to undo the buttons on her dress.

"We can always do this another time," she says, teasing. "If you'd rather go back to your wife? Back to the lovely Paula?"

*

It's the same dress she'd been wearing at the Gregsons' party when they'd first met a couple of weeks earlier. Paula hadn't said anything, not a word all afternoon, but as soon as they'd pulled out of the Gregsons' driveway, heading home, she turned to him and said, "So, what did *you* think of it?"

"Think of what?" he said.

"Her *dress*. Hannah's dress."

He kept his eyes on the road, thankful he didn't have to look at her.

"What do you mean?" he said.

Paula watched the trees fly by, the patchwork of yellow and green fields stretching as far as she could see. "It's okay," she said. "I'm not *blaming* you." She reached over and placed her hand on his knee. Left it there, like she hadn't decided what to do with it yet. "To be fair," she said, "I think *I'd* wear a dress like that if I looked like Hannah. If *I* had those legs."

She shook her head. "Fucking whore. Fucking *men*."

He nodded, but knew it would be counterproductive to say anything.

"I thought Nick was going to start dribbling," Paula said. "I mean, *actually* start dribbling." She squeezed his knee and removed her hand. "Did you see him? *Drooling*. Like one of those dogs, you know, those horrible, *disgusting* dogs that slobber all over the place."

*

He feels a sneeze coming on, the same twitch he felt last time, and slips the mask over his head. The elastic's tight, a lot tighter than he would have liked. One size fits all, it had said on the box, but they were Japanese. *Made in Kyoto*, it said, in big red letters. He should have factored that in. Should have looked closer to home, for a supplier that catered to larger, European-sized heads.

He pulls his shorts down and almost loses his balance when they get tangled around his swollen ankles. He kicks the shorts away and breathes deeply.

"That's better," he says through the mask. The twitch has gone, and the cloying sweetness of the rapeseed with it. His voice comes out a little muffled, as if it belongs to someone else, and he likes that. If he's someone else, he reasons, then that should, logically, absolve him of all blame for what he's about to do.

He looks down at Hannah and says, "Yes, that's much, much better."

City Lights

Thirty-three floors up, and she can see the whole world. From here, she thinks, everything is possible. This wasn't always the case. She used to hold on to him when the planes came in. Too close, skimming over roofs. She'd freeze, feel the building sway.

He made fun of her. Told her it was supposed to do that, to give, to bend. If it didn't, he said, it would snap in two and then where would we be? I'll tell you, he said. Fucked, that's where we'd be.

He'd lived on the forty-seventh floor before he'd moved in with her. Now *that* was something, he said. You can see *everything* up there. Not just the airport, the planes coming and going, but the harbour and the mountains and the distant lights of another country.

Sometimes, at night, she climbs up on to the windowsill and leans out. It's a long way down and there's nothing to stop her falling. But she sits there, on the ledge, and smokes a cigarette. It doesn't bother her now, when the building moves and sways. She looks out across the city lights, wondering if he's still out there somewhere.

Fifteen Minutes

Sit tight, his mother says, and don't you worry about a thing. She leans forward, whispers everything is going to be okay, and kisses him on the head. Ethan isn't worried, but his mother is shaking, her voice breaking. He knows she's been crying because her big brown eyes are red and puffy. He nods. He wants to cry too, but he's older now and he has to be all grown-up and sensible, just for her. He'd do anything for her. She kisses him again and steps back before closing the door on him.

He hears her fumbling with the key, stabbing it into the keyhole and missing, poking at it, when all she needs to do is slide it into the hole and turn it once to the right. He can hear her, talking to herself, her breathing heavy, exasperated. She drops the key and hisses when it bounces off the hardwood floor. She always drops the key. All fingers and thumbs.

He doesn't mind the dark. It's not *dark* dark anyway, not once his eyes get used to it. There's a thin strip of light at the bottom of the door. Not much, but enough to make out a few blurred shapes: the shoe rack, the mop and bucket, the winter coats hanging from the pegs. Old toys he's outgrown: the ones his mother can't bring herself to throw away.

His mother has given him a cushion to sit on and

a blanket to keep him warm. She said they won't be long. Fifteen minutes. *Just sit tight, son, and try to be quiet. Can you do that?* Ethan had nodded, said he'd be quiet as a mouse.

He listens to his mother's footsteps as she hurries, in her high heels, down the hallway. He knows what she's like, how much she worries about him. He knows she'll stop outside the bedroom door and look back over her shoulder. Check on him one last time. He hears the bedroom door opening and closing. Hears voices. His mother's, soft, scared, and *his. He* does most of the talking. When he shouts, Ethan can feel the walls shake, like the whole house is going to come crashing down.

Ethan covers his ears with his hands and buries his head between his knees. But he can still hear him, the shouting, the grunts and groans. Then nothing. Then his mother sobbing.

Heavy Lifting

She gives me directions to her new place and tells me to pull the van up on to the pavement, close as I can get to the front door. It's going to be a bugger, she says, leaning over, her hand on my lap. Getting the boxes in, she says, and all that furniture too.

There's no sign of Barry, even though he's supposed to meet us there to help with the heavy lifting.

Barry is the new me, my replacement. My wife, technically she's still my wife, says Barry's a terrible fuck, a really terrible fuck, and this makes me feel a little better, but not much. I've seen Barry. He's a fat slob, a retired accountant. I could have kicked the crap out of him, *should* have kicked the crap out of him. Maybe I will kick the crap out of him, next time I see him. If he ever turns up.

"It's nothing personal," she says, out of nowhere. She's looking straight ahead, down the street. It's a nice street, leafy, with trees on either side and a church on the corner.

"Well, it is," I say. "It *is* personal."

"You know what I mean," she says. She examines her fingernails, her perfectly manicured blood-red nails. They're like talons. Sharp enough to tear through flesh.

I kill the engine and we sit in silence. I watch her

out of the corner of my eye. The leopard-print mini-skirt, the long legs. Not bad, I used to tell her. Not bad at all for an old girl on the wrong side of sixty.

"You'll not be lifting much in those," I say, meaning her high heels.

She looks down and wiggles her painted toes. She places a hand on my knee and gives me that look.

"Maybe you should get started," she says.

"What about Barry?"

"What about him?"

"He's supposed to be here, to help."

"You're probably better off doing it yourself," she says.

She wiggles her toes again.

"Better make a start," she says. "I don't want to sit here all day."

Him off the Telly

She says he reminds her of that bloke off the telly.

"You *know*," she says, her hand on his knee. She'd tried to undo his zip earlier, copped a quick feel but stopped when she snagged a finger. "Whatshisname," she says. "You know, him with the teeth."

He catches the barman's eye and orders her another drink. A double this time, and a bag of pork scratchings.

"It's my birthday today," she says. She swivels the chair to face him, her pointy knees stabbing him.

"It is?" They'd been talking for an hour and she'd never mentioned anything about a birthday. He raises his glass. "Happy birthday," he says.

She hiccups. "It's not really. Not really my birthday." She grins. "It was though."

"When?"

She shrugs her shoulders. "Oh, *I* don't know." Her shoulders are just as pointy as her knees. Like they could cause some damage. "Last month, I *think*. What month is it?"

He doesn't ask how old she is. If he was pushed, he'd say mid-fifties, but the lighting's not great. She could be anything.

Instead, he asks her about the bloke off the telly.

"He was in that thing," she says. "You *know*, that

thing that was on a while ago. That thing on the telly."

"I don't think I saw it," he says. "I never really watch the telly." He has an old black-and-white in his bedroom, perched high up on the wall next to the window, gathering dust. It's on all the time, day and night, but it's muted. There's a remote, somewhere, but he can't remember what he did with it.

"It was good," she says. "The thing." She finishes her drink and wipes her mouth with the back of her hand, all the way up to her elbow, the way a kid would. "But I don't like him. Him with the teeth."

She reaches for his zip again and says, "Anyway, he looks nothing like you, not really."

Last Night

There's an old double mattress in the skip, soggy and stained, but it'll do. He just needs to lie down for a while, till his head clears.

*

He hears something scraffling around in the bushes just as he's about to doze off. A badger, a fox. Sniffing around in the undergrowth. A rat maybe. He'd read something in the *Advertiser* the other day about rats: not just rats, but "mutant" rats, rats bigger than cats. There'd been a grainy photo of some gormless fuck who'd speared one with a pitchfork, holding it up to the camera like a big-game trophy hunter. Roy thought there was something off about it straight away: the angle, the perspective, the way the rat was held aloft, skewered on the end of the pitchfork like that. It *was* big, there was no getting away from it, but Roy didn't like being taken for a ride. He ripped the page out and scrunched it up. Would have called the paper and given them a right piece of his mind if he could have been bothered.

*

He wakes up in the early hours. He's wet himself, but it doesn't smell too bad this time. He rolls over, on to his back, and looks up at the stars. His head's still spinning from the drink, from last night, but he starts counting, left to right across the sky, even the little ones, the tiny little specks of distant light he can only see when he squints with his good eye. Sometimes in the pub, when he's had a few, he tells anyone who's listening what it's like up there. That there's two hundred billion galaxies up there, give or take, and that's just the ones we know about, the ones in the observable universe, and that some of those galaxies have a trillion stars, some more than a *hundred trillion*. He watches their faces as they try to wrap their stupid little heads around the numbers, the impossible to fathom numbers, and he knows what they're thinking: how does someone like you, someone full of shit like you, know something like that? He doesn't mind. People can say what they want. He just shrugs and says, How many can you see? How many of those stars can you see with the naked eye, right now, right up there in the sky? Go on, how many? And let's make it interesting. If you're wrong, it's your round, and mine's a pint of cider, thank you very much. A million, they say. Ten million. Fifty million. Some bright spark will say a billion. Roy smiles and shakes his head, and says, Couple of thousand. Four thousand tops. Now where's my cider?

*

Last night's a bit like his head, all blurry and fuzzy. But he remembers the bloke with the huge hands. The bloke with the bald head and fat neck. It's the hands that he remembers though. He'd never seen hands like that, big as shovels, grabbing him by the throat. Roy remembers struggling, his feet off the ground, trying to hit the bloke, scratch his eyes out, and then not struggling, and then nothing at all.

He's foggy on the details, but he thinks it might have had something to do with a woman. Something he'd said to her. He wouldn't be surprised if that's what it was all about it. He knows better than anyone what he's like when he's had a drink or two.

*

He's found that it's a lot easier to climb into a skip than it is to climb out. He does get out eventually, his feet sinking into the squishy mattress, via a not very complicated process of folding himself over the rusty lip of the skip and allowing gravity to do the rest.

He lands face first, in a puddle.

*

He rubs his head as he shuffles towards the nearest house. He picks at a scab just above his left ear. His hair is caked with blood; his ear feels hot and three times bigger than it should be.

*

He's pretty sure the house belongs to Marion. He's known Marion for years: knows she'll sort him out with a cuppa and some biscuits, let him put his feet up till he's right as rain.

He walks around the side of the house. The garden's a mess, the grass knee-high. This surprises him, knowing what Marion's like. He looks around, at the pink tricycle on the yard, at the wooden climbing frame at the bottom of the garden, and he senses something isn't quite right.

He knocks on the door and flinches. His knuckles are raw and there's a deep cut between his thumb and index finger. He remembers something else from last night: clenching his fist and taking a wild swing at Baldie, the bloke with the hands, just before everything went black. And a woman, in the background, snarling at him, shouting, Kill him, Tony, fucking kill him, wring his scrawny fucking neck.

*

Roy uses the heel of his hand instead, and thumps the door.

"Marion!" he shouts, peering into the frosted glass, into the kitchen. "Marion! Chance of a cup of tea, Marion?"

There's movement behind the glass, and the door opens.

"Marion?" he asks, swaying.

The kid's ten, maybe eleven. Long hair, glasses. Could be younger, or older. Roy doesn't even know if it's a boy or girl, what with all that hair.

"Who the fuck are you?" the kid says.

Roy stumbles and tries not to fall over. "Who the fuck are *you*?" he says. "You're not—"

*

The kid turns and squeals, "Dad!"

The dad appears instantly, as if by magic. Maybe he's been there all the time and Roy has only just clocked him.

"What the fuck do you want?" he says. He's got long hair, too, all the way down past his shoulders, but he's thin and wispy on top. He's not much to look at but he's got tattoos.

"Where's Marion?" Roy asks.

"Who the—"

"I just want a cup of tea," Roy says, "and some biscuits. I—"

He barges into the kitchen. "Go and get Marion," he says, "and tell her to put the kettle on."

*

Roy smiles.

He swallows some blood and thinks he might have lost a tooth or two.

That fucking kid.

Roy'd been so busy watching the dad that he'd forgotten about the kid. He had to hand it to the little fucker, though, sucker-punching him like that. Right in the mouth. A one-way ticket to la-la land.

*

The grass is wet, the ground soft and spongy. There are no stars now, just a grey smudge of sky, like dirty cotton wool. Roy starts counting anyway, and thinks it probably wouldn't be the worst thing in the world if he could just lie there a while longer, lost in the grass, counting the stars he can't see.

Hairy Mary

Sometimes, when they're talking or watching TV or sitting in the car looking out across the sea, she runs the tip of her tongue over it, making it moist, then patting it down with her finger. Tending to it, nurturing it, as if it were a small pet or a houseplant. Sometimes, he thinks, she doesn't even know she's doing it. She'll do it in her sleep, when she's deep in a book. But sometimes, when they're out and about, in a bar or a café, as they are now, she knows exactly what she's doing, and she'll stroke it, ever so slowly, and run her finger over it. If someone's watching, as the heavily made-up woman at the next table is watching her now, she'll quite happily put on a little performance and have some fun with it.

"Some of the names they used to call me," she says, her foot caressing his under the table. "Tash. Chewbacca. *Hairy Mary*." She raises her bushy eyebrows to the ceiling. "I mean, come *on*, how funny is *that*?"

"Hilarious," he says. The woman at the next table had been watching them sideways, spying on them over the menu. Now, she's just staring.

"Do you mind if I *tickle* it?" he says.

She juts her chin out. "Be my guest."

He tickles her moustache and says, "It's so soft, so *luxuriant*."

"I like to call him my little furry friend," she says, laughing. "There was a time, really, when he was my *only* friend. There was this one girl, right. Sonia Caffey. She was a right cow. Horrible, she was. Used to tease me *all* the time, used to call me Monkey Face and get all the other girls to make monkey noises at the bus stop in the morning. Break time, too, all day long. Even at the bus stop at night."

She shrugs and wets her lip. "But it's okay," she says, smiling, looking at the woman at the next table. "You know what girls are like."

Lunch

"I'll take the spare room," Jake said, poking his fork at his cold food. "Or the sofa. I don't mind."

Claire shook her head. "Jill said I could crash at hers. Till I find something else."

Jake looked away, towards the old man at the corner table. He wouldn't have noticed him, wouldn't have given him a second look if he had, but the old man was whistling to himself. On and off, a few bars of something Jake didn't recognise. Something jaunty. Like the old bastard didn't have a care in the world.

Claire hoped Jake wouldn't make a scene. "I'll keep paying the mortgage," she said. "Till we, you know. Till we sort things out." She didn't tell him she'd already paid a deposit on a converted warehouse down by the harbour. That she'd cut an extra set of keys for Alec.

Jake hadn't thought about the mortgage. How he'd manage without her money, how he'd pay the bills and everything else.

"You think he's doing that on purpose?" Jake said. He turned to Claire, then back to the old man. "Winding me up like that?"

Claire didn't say anything. Not saying anything was usually the best thing to do when he was like that.

"I mean, for fuck's sake, he—"

The old man cut him off with another short burst. A different tune this time. Higher pitched. Jake knew this one but couldn't put a name to it, not yet. The waitress didn't seem to mind, Jake noticed, smiling to herself as she walked past the old man's table. She was new, this one: thickset, with red hair and a funny accent. Russian or Polish or something. She'd caught Jake looking at her tits when she showed them to their table. He wasn't gawping or anything, so he didn't know what her problem was. They were just there, and they *were* nice tits, *very* nice tits actually, so it's not like he'd done anything wrong.

"I think he is," Jake said, "I think the old bastard's doing that on purpose. Being all fucking happy like that."

"Just ignore him," Claire said.

Jake dropped the fork on to the plate.

"I'm sorry," he said, and got up, brushing her hand aside.

Whereabouts Unknown

He was the speccy kid, before he had his eyes fixed.
The fat kid before he joined the gym. Taxi Doors
before he had his lugs pinned back. Now, when he
looks in the mirror, he sometimes forgets who he
is, what he used to look like. His mum blames the
money, says he's got more bloody money than sense.
Says it's made him soft and stupid in the head. She
liked his ears just the way they were before. "Your
dad," she says, "he must be spinning in his grave,
the sight of you." He reminds her his dad's not dead,
that he scarpered when he was nine. A week after his
ninth birthday in fact. Disappeared in the wee hours
with the woman from the post office. Gone, just like
that. Whereabouts unknown.

Later, he'd heard they'd headed south, to
Manchester or Liverpool. Somewhere like that,
somewhere big and industrial and far off. He doesn't
tell his mum that he'd been trying to find his dad ever
since. That a few years ago he tracked him down to a
three-bed semi on the outskirts of Preston, that he'd
parked up at the end of a grim-looking road and sat
there in the car for hours, waiting. He doesn't tell her
he saw him. His dad and his new family, the woman
from the post office. He assumes it was the woman
from the post office, but he can't remember what she

looked like back then and couldn't imagine what the years might have done to her even if he had. It didn't matter. He was with a woman, that's all. And there was a kid. The kid was young, eight or nine, the same age he'd been all those years ago. The kid even looked like him. The big ears and the glasses. Like looking at an old photo of himself.

He'd climbed out of the car, a thousand rehearsed lines rushing through his head. So many things to say and no idea how to say them. He didn't even know why he was there. Some kind of closure, probably. That's what they called it nowadays, wasn't it? *Closure*. A big, fat full stop at the end of it all.

It wouldn't have taken much. A simple "hello" to begin with. The rest, he thinks, would have taken care of itself. But he turned, his head down, and walked off in the other direction. Kept on walking, through a park full of dog shit and discarded cigarettes, past a row of boarded-up shopfronts, till he was back where he'd started, his car sitting there waiting for him, ready to take him home.

He doesn't tell his mum any of this. Maybe she's right. Maybe it's better he's dead, spinning in his grave.

The Woman from the Council

It's about six feet high and seventy feet long. About two feet thick. Reasonably well tended. To the untrained eye, it's a normal, common or garden hedge. But woman from the council knows otherwise.

She takes a tape measure out of her pocket and she measures it. She smiles. As she suspected. There's an overhang, a protuberance of exactly eight and three-quarter inches. She steps back, pleased with herself. Takes her clipboard out of her bag and makes some notes. She can't wait to get home to write up her report, to get the ball rolling. She'll be back tomorrow, first thing in the morning, to take photographic evidence for the enforcement officer. She'll email the enforcement officer once she's completed her report. Let him know it's coming. Forewarned and forearmed, and all that. He's an old friend, the enforcement officer, and he often jokes he'd be out of a job if it weren't for her. For people like her.

She knows they're watching her, the residents. She saw the curtains twitch when she arrived. Upstairs window, the bedroom overlooking the back garden. Dirty-grey curtains. She's heard they're a funny lot. Shifty, not from round here. Probably up to no good.

She knows what they all say about her, behind her back. About the woman from the council and her tape measure and clipboard. About her dogged determination to stick her nose into other people's business. She's heard all the accusations and rumours, that she can be somewhat economical with the truth, that she may, on occasion, have overestimated her expense claims. She doesn't care. It's *her* village and it might *only* be a hedge. But she knows what these people are like. She won't have it. She won't allow things to slip, to fester.

Diamondback

He met her near the lion enclosure. Stood next to her for a long time before he said anything, as they watched two females through the smudged Plexiglass.

"Magnificent, aren't they?" he said.

She didn't say anything, so he said it again. "Magnificent creatures." He inched closer to her. "It says on the plaque there that the male, wherever he is, weighs around 450 pounds." He said it again, to himself. *Four hundred and fifty pounds*. "That's, what, more than thirty stone. Nearly three of me."

"Are you some kind of weirdo?" she said, not looking at him. She was chewing green bubblegum, blowing tiny little bubbles that didn't amount to anything.

"Probably," he said. "But we're all a bit weird, aren't we?"

She turned to him and blew another bubble. "Speak for yourself," she said.

*

He said, "I don't even know your name."

They'd moved on to the tigers.

"Maybe they're inside," she said, on tiptoes, trying to get a better view.

"I'm Gabriel," he said. He offered his hand. Slipped it back into his pocket when she ignored it.

*

"Do you want to see the giraffes?" he asked. The giraffes were his favourites. She'd already walked off and he had to hurry to catch up with her.

"Giraffes are boring," she said. She stopped and blew a bubble. "Don't you think?"

"I *love* giraffes."

"You do?"

She offered him some bubblegum.

"It's my last piece," she said. "But you can have it."

*

He bought a coffee from a kiosk near the penguin pool. She bought more bubblegum (five packets) and a peppermint tea. The penguin pool was empty except for a guy in overalls hosing it down.

"Where's the penguins?" Gabriel shouted, looking down.

The guy looked up, a cigarette hanging out the corner of his mouth.

"You what?"

"The penguins? Where are the penguins?"

The guy shook his head and said, "How the fuck should I know?"

*

She said her name was Valerie but everyone called her Val.

Gabriel offered his hand.

"Gabriel," he said.

Val looked at his hand and smiled, and walked off, towards the creepy-crawly house.

They had to wait outside in the sun while a party of tiny schoolchildren filed out one by one, each tethered to the next with a bright orange wrist strap, like miniature beacons in their high-vis bibs.

Gabriel nodded at the red-faced teacher bringing up the rear. He remembered coming here when he was a kid, the teachers taking turns to keep an eye on them while they nipped off for a quick fag. No safety straps and shiny bibs in those days. They had to hold hands, sometimes, the kids. They'd each pair off with their best pal, but there was always an odd number, always one left over. Always Gabriel. He'd shrug, pretend it was no big deal, and take the teacher's hand.

*

Gabriel liked to close his eyes and pretend he was dead. He loved creepy-crawlies almost as much as he loved giraffes.

"Watch," he said, his eyes tight shut. He could smell the wet earth, could feel the beetles and worms and spiders all around him, wriggling, chirping, humming. "This is what it's going to be like," he said, "when we're dead, when we're six foot under. We—"

"Come here," Val said.

Gabriel blinked, waited till his eyes refocused. Val was trying to jimmy a door in one of the glass tanks that lined the wall.

"Should you be doing that?" Gabriel said. "I mean—"

"Nearly there," she said, working the lock with the tip of a penknife. "The trick is not to force it," she said. "Get it right and you don't have to break it, you just—"

The lock clicked and Val turned.

"Like that," she said, grinning.

"But—"

He watched her roll up her sleeve and reach into the tank, all the way into the back.

"Look," she said, offering her hand up to him.

"What is it?"

"That," Val said, "is a diamondback moth."

"You can't—"

"Plutella xylostella, to give him his proper name. Isn't he beautiful? Go on, take him."

Gabriel moved closer but the moth fluttered away like a fleck of dust caught in the wind.

Val looked up to the ceiling. He thought she'd be furious with him, but she was smiling. "He's free now," she said. "You see him?"

Gabriel looked up but couldn't see a thing, except for the blinking red eye of the CCTV camera above the exit.

"We should probably get going," Val said, grabbing his hand. "They said they'd press charges next time they caught me."

Eggs

I start thinking about it on my way back from work, how things haven't turned out the way I'd hoped. About my wife having a fat ass and my three kids hating me.

By the time I get home, I've already made up my mind.

My wife's in the dining room and the middle kid is sitting next to her, doing his homework.

"I'm leaving," I say from the hallway. "I'm heading for the fucking woods."

My wife ignores me, and so does the middle kid. There's no sign of the other two kids, the older one with the gormless face and the youngest one, my daughter. She's pretty gormless too but not as gormless as the older one.

I run up the stairs and throw some things into a rucksack. I grab a pillow on the way out of the bedroom because I figure a big fluffy pillow will come in quite handy. When I come back downstairs, my wife with the fat ass and the middle kid are still doing the homework, my wife sitting with her chin resting on her hand, staring at the wall. The middle kid, whose name I sometimes forget, is droning on about coordinating conjunctions in that whiny, nasal little voice of his.

I poke my head around the door and say, "I'll be off then."

My wife looks up as if she's just awoken from a deep sleep and says, "What?"

"I said I'm off." I show her the rucksack and the pillow, like I mean it this time.

She shrugs and goes back to staring at the wall. The middle kid doesn't say anything at all, which doesn't surprise me because he hates me, because they all hate me.

I take the van. The car would have been better but the van has a mattress in the back, the one I've been meaning to drop off at the tip for I can't remember how long, and some bits and bobs that might come in useful when I'm out there in the wild. My toolbox, a groundsheet, a stepladder. That sort of thing.

I drive for a long time, the village disappearing in the rear-view mirror till it's nothing but a distant blur, a bad memory. There's a picnic area a mile or so into the woods, a clearing with benches and a squat red-brick toilet block, but I keep going, deeper and deeper till the temperature drops and the air smells wet and heavy.

A few miles further on I meet a man selling eggs.

"Best eggs for miles around," he says. "Do you want some?"

He holds one up for inspection. It's brown, medium-sized, the kind of thing you'd buy from the supermarket.

"I'll have four," I say. I don't even like eggs. "Second thoughts, make it six."

He says he's only got three. He gives me the egg

he's been holding in his muddy hand and produces another two from his inside pocket. They're also brown, but slightly smaller than the first one.

I grab some change from the dashboard, count it quickly and hand it over to him. "Take it," I say. "That's two quid and seventeen pence. I have no need for money, not now."

I start telling him about my wife with the fat ass and the kids who hate me, about how I'm going to start a new life in the woods and fashion a shelter out of oak branches and spruce boughs and feast on woodland creatures.

But he nods and walks off, the spare change rattling in his pocket, and I'm left sitting there holding the eggs.

I watch him in the side mirror as he tramples through the long grass before being swallowed up by the woods. When I look down, I realise one of the eggs has leaked and there's a wet patch around my crotch.

Finite

He'd read in the paper that everyone is born with an allocated number of heartbeats. He thinks it was in the paper, or maybe he'd heard it in the pub or from one of the lads at work. It was true, anyway. He didn't know how many he'd been given or how many he had left, but he'd decided that was that, he was going to sit put and make the most of them.

"Stands to reason, doesn't it," he said, putting his feet up. "All that running around, using up all those heartbeats you're not going to get back."

His wife was ready to go, wanted to get going to beat the traffic.

"I'm not budging," he said. He'd slowed his breathing. In, out, nice and easy. No point in wasting them. He didn't want to go to the shops anyway. Thing like that, traipsing around all over the place, he'd lose hundreds, probably thousands, of heartbeats. Heartbeats he'd rather keep for himself, for a rainy day.

"So what're you going to do?" his wife said. "Sit there and die?"

"I'm not budging," he said. "I'm not." He had to stay calm. He felt for his pulse, and counted his life slipping away from him one beat at a time.

The Monster

Chris sits at the next table, three or four feet from the man who murdered his mother. He's older now, the man who murdered his mother. Well into his sixties, the same age his mother would have been. Not *that* old, Chris thinks. But the years haven't been good to him, to the man who murdered his mother.

He's got a name, this man. It's a disappointingly normal name, but Chris can't bring himself to say it, even now. The papers called him the Monster. Chris thinks it's too obvious, a cheap headline to appeal to the lowest common denominator. To sell a few more papers. But the name stuck. Chris still has the cuttings somewhere, in a scrapbook in a long-unopened drawer. There was this one cutting in particular: a grainy black-and-white photo of a big man with a wide face and dark hair. Chris used to take it out and study it, used it to carry it around with him and stare at it till his eyes hurt, looking for something, for some meaning. But it told him nothing. It was just a photo.

*

Chris has been watching him for a while now, the man who murdered his mother. At a distance initially, but closing in bit by bit. Ever-decreasing circles. This is the closest he's been to him. Three or four feet. Touching distance.

The thing that strikes Chris now is how old the Monster looks. How the years have reduced him, how they have taken everything from him. He likes to think it's the guilt that's done it, but he knows that's not the case.

"You know what she were like," the Monster says.

The Monster's friends nod sympathetically into their pints. This is the other thing that surprises Chris: that the Monster, the man who murdered his mother, the man who did all those things to her, still has friends.

"No bloody angel," someone says. The others murmur, nod their old heads.

"I'll drink to that," another says.

Chris looks into the Monster's eyes. The Monster looks right back at him. Right through him. Just another lonely guy in the pub. Not one of them, not a friend, but not a threat either.

*

Chris lets himself in through the back door, with the key the Monster keeps under the cracked flowerpot.

He knows the house well. He's been here before, on more than a few occasions. He knew this day was coming, that he had to be ready.

He looks in the Monster's fridge. It's empty, as usual, except for a bottle of milk, a slab of bright orange cheese which might, he thinks, be the same slab of cheese from last time. Three cans of beer too. Chris helps himself to one. He gulps down half of it and pours the rest out on to the floor. He looks down, watches it splatter and fizz, before he throws the bottle into the sink. The bottle bounces and ricochets out of the sink and lands on the draining board, spinning.

*

Sometimes he likes to sit in the Monster's armchair. It sags in the middle and the armrests are worn right through, but it's comfortable, and sometimes he thinks he could just sit there and close his eyes and nod off and not have to worry about anything ever again.

Tonight, though, he sits in the corner. On the floor, his back against the cold wall.

He makes himself as small as possible in the darkness, and waits for the man who murdered his mother.

Nod

Bit of fresh air, they thought. That'll do the trick. So they took him down to Bamburgh, to the beach. Parked near Stag Rock so they didn't have to walk far. He nodded off soon as he lowered himself into the deckchair.

Maybe some sun, they thought. That's what he needed. Bit of vitamin D. They raked the leaves off the grass and told him to soak up some rays. He keeled right over, face first. His hands still in his pockets.

The doctor said it might be narcolepsy. Said she'd take some blood and run some tests. Gave them a number for a support group before ushering them out and washing her hands.

They took him to the support group, but it was warm and stuffy in the church hall and he dozed off in a flimsy chair. He went over backwards, feet in the air. Landed in a heap and didn't wake up.

His wife looked down at him. Saw his chest rise and fall. He wasn't old, had the heart of a lion, despite everything. She was convinced he was going to live forever, or she had been. She turned to the group leader and said, "What should I do?"

The group leader smiled and said, "You don't need to do anything." They both looked down. "My wife," he said, "she's been doing this for years. In front of the telly, at work, in the shower. Just like that, lights out."

He saw that she was crying. He took her hand and said, "You'll get used to it."

He rubbed her hand, a little too familiarly, she thought, and said, "What I like to do, with my wife, is just to give her a little poke. A little poke, or a pinch of the skin. Behind her arm's good, or in the crook of her neck, you know. Just to make sure she's still breathing."

He let go of her hand and smiled again. "If they're breathing, then leave them alone." He looked down at her husband and said, "Don't you worry, he'll wake up when he's ready. All in good time."

Home

"It's me."

"Oh."

"Hello."

"Hello. Where are you?"

"The Garden."

"Nice."

"Not really."

"How come?"

"It's hot, it's like a fucking greenhouse."

"It *is* a greenhouse. Sort of."

"You know what I mean. Fucking tourists, fucking everywhere."

"Why don't you go somewhere else? The tree house. The cherry orchard. It's nice up there, up in the orchard. Cooler, not so busy."

"I can't."

"Why not?"

"You know why not. All that pollen up there, all those flowers and trees and shit. I've already sneezed a million times and I've only been here five minutes. Anyway, I've just bought a coffee."

"How is it?

"Bitter. Burnt. And the table's wobbly, and covered in bird shit. The waitress said sorry, said she'd come and clean it up but looks like she's buggered off. Fucking pigeons, they're fucking everywhere. I tell you, if one of those little bastards comes anywhere near me—"

"Why don't you move? To another table?"

"Cos it's heaving. Fucking tourists. And there's a bunch of kids, a busload of them, just arrived. They're heading this way, the noisy little fuckers. And there's this woman at the next table, she's got a mouth like a fucking foghorn, keeps saying the same thing over and over. It's really doing my head in."

"What do you mean, the same thing over and over?"

"What do you think I mean? She's on the phone and she's just said, 'Absolutely, absolutely, *absolutely*'. Just like that, really emphasising the last word, you know, every fucking time. 'That's amazing, that's amazing, that's *amazing*.' Christ all fucking mighty, and it's so *hot* in here."

"Why don't you come home?"

"Because I'm supposed to be writing."

"You're writing again?"

"Supposed to be."

"That's great."

"It's not."

"How's it going?"

"It's not. It's not going at all."

"How come?"

"I don't know. I … I don't know. It's just not. It's shit."

"You always say that."

"Because it's always shit."

"That's not true."

"It is."

"It's not, and you know it's not. You need to stop putting yourself down."

"But it's shit."

"It's not."

"It is."

"You're being silly now."

"I don't care."

"Come home."

"Home?"

"Yes."

"You've changed your tune. You told me to fuck off. Remember?"

"I didn't—"

"That's what you said. That's *exactly* what you said. *Fuck off. For good this time.*"

"That was last week."

"And now?"

"Just come home. We can talk."

"I don't know."

"Come home, or I'm going to hang up."

"I'm writing."

"You said that."

"Okay."

"Okay what?"

"I don't know."

Houdini

She read a lot. You'd see her around campus, on her own, hunched over a book.

"Houdini," was the first thing she said to you. You were sitting nearby, on the steps in the main court-yard. It took you a while to realise she was talking to you.

"Houdini?" you said. "What about him?"

She looked over to you, her eyes scrunched up against the sun. "You know how he died?"

You said you didn't. Drowned? Asphyxiated?

"Punched in the gut," she said. "Someone *punched* him in the gut and killed him. Can you believe that?"

*

She took a year off. When she came back for the final year she wouldn't say where she'd been.

"It's not important," she said. "Just let it go."

She handed you her kimono as she stepped into the bath. "Ask me again and I'm leaving."

You watched her slip into the cold water, her skin pale and goosebumped.

She took a deep breath, held it for five seconds, then exhaled slowly. She did that three times and nodded on her final inhale. Your signal. You started the timer and watched as she slid under the water, one eye open, watching you.

Her record was three minutes and seven seconds. You'd tried it yourself once, not wanting to show off or anything, and not wanting to get too close to her record because you knew how much it meant to her. You managed a minute.

"Houdini," she said, eyes wide with admiration. "He did *eleven* minutes."

*

She took a vow of silence when you moved in together.

When you asked why, she shrugged, tight-lipped.

"How long?" you asked.

She shrugged again.

"Come on," you said. "This isn't funny any more."

She handed you a pad and pencil. She put her finger to her mouth to hush you, and pointed at the pad.

"You're serious, aren't you?"

She nodded and pointed again.

You wrote, *You're fucking nuts!* You added another exclamation mark, and did it with such force that the pencil snapped in two.

*

You don't know what happened to her. You heard she left again, after you moved out. You still have an old address somewhere and you could probably track her down. Facebook her, Google her, ask around. But you remember what she used to say, about things not being important, about letting things go.

You think back to that first time you talked to her on the courtyard steps, and you let her go.

Sandcastles

She likes to stop in the park on the way home and watch the kids playing on the swings, messing around in the sandpit. It's quiet today, the mid-afternoon lull, but there's a young mum on the next bench.

Sarah says, "He's beautiful." She smiles at the woman, then at the little boy playing in the sand.

Sarah's good at small talk. She can't remember the last time she talked to anyone she knows, to anyone who knows the weight of her history, but give her a stranger, a clean slate, and she can blabber on all day.

"So well behaved," she says. The little boy is trying to build a castle, but the sand's too dry, too fine, and the walls crumble as soon as he lifts the upturned bucket.

"I think it needs some water," Sarah says. "To wet the sand. To make it all mushy."

It's usually the mums she talks to. Tired, distracted mums with that faraway look. The dads too. But the dads don't say as much. They tend to avoid eye contact. Would rather just sit there and fiddle with their phones than talk to her.

The little boy's name is Harvey, the mum says. Almost four.

"He'll be starting school in September," she says.

"Reception class." She shakes her head, as if she can't quite believe it herself.

Sarah nods. "It goes so fast," she says. "I remember wishing I had a penny every time someone said that to me." She looks out across the park, towards the pond. They've fenced it off now. A chain-link fence to keep the kids out, to keep them from harm. They put up a red-and-white sign, warning parents to be vigilant. Sarah remembers how cold the water was, how black. Coming up for air, forcing herself under again, knowing he was already gone.

"My son's nineteen now," she says.

The mum nods, but looks away.

"At university," Sarah says.

It's not a complete lie, she tells herself. He would have been nineteen, and she knows he would have gone to college, to university, because he'd been ever so clever, such a bright boy. All the teachers used to say that, how clever he was.

She turns back to the little boy and watches another sandcastle crumble.

Sink

That was when she caught him urinating in the kitchen sink.

"What?" he said. He looked out the window, at the rain bouncing off the backyard, as he zipped himself up.

She was in the doorway, halfway between dining room and kitchen, a heavy bag of shopping in each hand. "How long've you been doing that?" she said.

"What?"

"*That.*"

He shrugged. He'd dribbled on the floor, but only a little bit, and wiped it away with his sock. He rarely went upstairs these days. They had a big old house, way too big for just the pair of them, and lots of stairs, and sometimes he just found it easier to use the sink. He thought she knew. Thought it was one of those things that was known and understood and not talked about.

She dropped the bags on to the tiled floor. One of the bags landed with a heavy thud. The other with a pop of broken glass.

"You filthy fucking pig," she said.

He washed his hands under the cold tap, smiling to himself. Tried to imagine the look on her face if he told her he sometimes nipped outside for a shit. Way

137

down at the bottom of the garden, in the narrow gap between the shed and next door's fence.

*

He heard her stomping around upstairs, clomping around like a bull elephant. She'd left a few times before. Usually a couple of days, sometimes a week. Once, last year, she was gone for a whole fortnight.

When he got to the top of the stairs, she was in the bedroom, the suitcase splayed out on the bed.

"What are you doing?" he said, catching his breath. Those fucking stairs.

She'd grabbed a few things, some underwear, some shirts, a big winter coat from the wardrobe.

"What do you think I'm doing?" she said, slamming the suitcase shut.

It was the old suitcase, the one they used to take on holiday with them when they still went on holidays together. It had been a good one but had seen better days.

"Do you want a hand?" he asked.

The zip had always been a bit of a bastard, a two-man job.

"Come here," he said. He closed the case and sat on the top of it, pressing his weight down while she reached for the zip.

"We should buy a new one," he said. "One of those nice ones, you know. The matching set."

She ignored him and waited for him to move.

"I'll say sorry," he said. "If you want me to. For … you know. For everything."

She grabbed the case and dragged it downstairs.

He wondered what else she had in there and how long she was planning to leave for this time.

"Do you want me to give you a lift?" he asked. "Or call a taxi or something?"

She was already halfway out, but reached back in for the keys.

"No need," she said, not looking at him. "I'm taking the car."

My Wife Left Me

My third wife, the one with the overactive thyroid, left me for another woman. I cried for a week. Something like that, it knocks a man off his stride. Fairly discombobulates you. But then I spotted an opportunity.

"You want to watch?" she said. "Watch what?"

I did that thing with my eyebrows. "*You* know." I did the eyebrow thing again. "If you don't mind."

She said she'd have to think about it. Have to get back to me after she'd had a word with Mo (Mo being the other woman).

She called back five days later. It was first thing in the morning and I was still in bed, alone, crying. She apologised and said she would have called earlier but the thyroid had been playing up again. The stress and everything. She said the doc had given her some new pills, to take on top of the carbimazole, and there'd been a reaction. Given her a right head, she said, and the scratching, don't talk to me about the fucking scratching. Everywhere, she said, and she meant *everywhere*: arms and legs, all her nooks and crannies. She blabbered on for a while and said she's going back to the doctor, but private this time, and by the way, Mo said no.

*

I tell him my third wife left me for another woman. He pauses, half-undressed, and says, "Sorry, man, that's really fucked up." His name's Russell and he's got a ponytail. He looks like he's in his late forties. I shrug. All stoic and everything. I don't tell him I cried for a week and then asked if I could watch. That my wife's new partner said no, that Mo said no, that I was a dirty fucking pervert and she'd report me to the police if I ever came within five miles of her. I start to tell him about my wife's overactive thyroid and her rash and how she's been scratching like a leper, but Russell says, "I get it, man," and finishes undressing. He's got love handles and a big yellow bruise above his left knee. He stands there, hands on hips, like it's the most natural thing in the world.

"I get it," he says again. He rubs himself and cups his hairless balls in his hand. "You thought you'd give her a taste of her own medicine, right?" He grins. "Thought you'd see what it's like on the other side, right?"

I take a step back. "I suppose," I say. "I mean, I don't know, I—" I could run, I think. It's not too late to run. Through the door, down the corridor, past reception, up the alley and back into the world. Run like fuck and keep on running. But Russell takes my hand. It's warm, his grip firm. It seems I'm not going anywhere.

"Relax," he says. "I'll be gentle."

Acknowledgements

I would like to thank the following for their support and encouragement: Paul Beckman, Niles Reddick, Ashley Chantler, Tom Hazuka, Santino Prinzi, Paul D. Brazill, Gareth Spark, Paul Heatley, Cal Marcius, Alan Beard, Tom Leins, Aidan Thorn, Ray Hoskins and K.A. Laity.

Special thanks to Dana, Allan and Mark at Vagabond, for everything.

Stories

Some of these stories have appeared in slightly different form in the following publications: "It Waits", "Uncle Colin" and "On Reflection We've Decided We're Going to Keep You" in *The Pygmy Giant*, "Crepuscular" and "The Fourth Wife" in *Flash: The International Short-Short Story Magazine*, "Body Parts", "In the Event of a Zombie Apocalypse" in *81words*, "Diversionary Purchases" in *FlashFlood/ National Flash Fiction Day*, "The Woods" in *Out of the Gutter*, "The Island" in *Spelk Fiction*, "Terms and Conditions" in *Near to the Knuckle*, and "Unfinished Business" in *Postcard Shorts*.

Ce livre apparti

Nom : _____

_____

Adresse : _____

_____

_____

Offert par :

_____

le _____ 200...

martine
la nouvelle élève

d'après les albums de Gilbert Delahaye et Marcel Marlier

Le jour de la rentrée, tout
le monde se retrouve dans
la cour de l'école.

— Qu'y a-t-il dans ton
panier ? demande Martine
à Stéphanie.

— C'est ma souris blanche.
Elle ne peut pas rester à la
maison à cause de
mon chat.

8

Martine n'a pas le
temps de parler plus
longtemps :
la maîtresse appelle
ses élèves.
Stéphanie cache
sa souris au-dessus
de l'armoire.

Martine fait la connaissance
de Cynthia, une nouvelle
élève. Elle est un peu perdue.
— Tu verras, la maîtresse est
gentille, la rassure Martine.
Suis-moi, je vais te guider.

— Je vous présente Cynthia,
dit la maîtresse à la classe.
Elle est Indienne.
Voilà une belle occasion de
faire un cours de géographie.
Qui sait où se trouve
l'Inde ?
— C'est en Asie, répond
François.

La maîtresse emmène
les élèves à la bibliothèque.
Dans la salle de lecture,
on ne s'ennuie jamais.

Il y a des albums illustrés,
des romans, des journaux...
Martine aimerait tout
emporter !

16

À la récréation, les élèves

jouent au ballon,

puis font la ronde.

— Viens avec nous,
dit Martine à Cynthia.
Tends les mains, on va faire
la toupie.

De retour en classe,
la maîtresse demande à
chacun d'écrire au directeur
d'un journal pour demander
l'autorisation de visiter son
imprimerie.

— Nous enverrons
les meilleurs textes, dit
la maîtresse.

Au cours de gymnastique,
on fait des roulades et
des sauts.

Emmanuel doit rester sur
un banc : il est tombé de
son vélo, et a le bras dans
le plâtre.

À midi, on mange à
la cantine. Chacun prend
son plateau.

— Tu as une nouvelle
copine ? demande
Emmanuel à Martine.

— Oui, elle vient
d'Inde, répond-elle en
l'aidant à couper sa viande.

Le repas est terminé,

et tout le monde se réunit

en atelier.

— Nous allons lire un

poème de Prévert, puis

nous l'illustrerons avec

des dessins, explique

la maîtresse. Qui veut

le raconter ?

— Moi ! dit Martine.

Ça commence en automne.

C'est l'histoire de deux

escargots qui vont voir leur

amie la feuille morte.

La pluie tombe, et le vent

souffle dans les arbres.

Les petits artistes
dessinent ensuite
l'histoire. Sophie,
très concentrée,
peint sur un chevalet.
— C'est joli,
dit Martine.

Quand tout est bien sec,
les dessins sont accrochés
aux murs de la classe.
Il y en a partout !

— On pourra les rapporter chez nous ? demande Sophie.

La classe se rend
maintenant à la rivière.
Avec une épuisette,
on récolte plein de
petits animaux !
— Oh, une grenouille !
s'exclame Martine.

De retour en classe,

on verse les têtards dans

l'aquarium.

— Quand ils auront bien grandi, nous les remettrons dans la rivière, dit la maîtresse.

Soudain,
la sonnerie
retentit.
On range rapidement
ses affaires. Stéphanie
n'oublie pas sa souris !

— Comme la journée
a passé vite !
À demain, Cynthia.
Martine se hâte de poster
la lettre au directeur
du journal.

http://www.casterman.com
D'après les personnages créés par Gilbert Delahaye et Marcel Marlier / Léaucour Création.
Imprimé en Chine. Dépôt légal : août 2009 ; D. 2009/0053/287.
Déposé au ministère de la Justice, Paris (loi n° 49.956 du 16 juillet 1949
sur les publications destinées à la jeunesse).
ISBN 978-2-203-02422-9